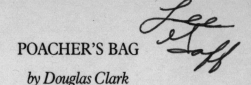

POACHER'S BAG

by Douglas Clark

"Another first-class contribution to his collection of mysteries. . . . Here . . . we have many of the classical elements of
the detective story."—*Daily Telegraph*

"Another of those cunningly convoluted detective stories
in which Clark excels."—*London Mystery Selection*

Also available in Perennial Library
by Douglas Clark:

ROAST EGGS

POACHER'S BAG

by

DOUGLAS CLARK

PERENNIAL LIBRARY
Harper & Row, Publishers
New York, Cambridge, Philadelphia, San Francisco
London, Mexico City, São Paulo, Sydney

A hardcover edition of this book was published by Victor Gollancz Ltd., London, England. It is here reprinted by arrangement with John Farquharson Ltd.

First PERENNIAL LIBRARY edition published 1983.

Library of Congress Cataloging in Publication Data

Clark, Douglas
    Poacher's bag.

    (Perennial library; P643)
    Reprint. Originally published: London : Gollancz, 1980.
    I. Title.
PR6053.L294P6   1983   823'.914   82-48810
ISBN 0-06-080643-5 (pbk.)

83   84   85   10   9   8   7   6   5   4   3   2   1

AUTHOR'S NOTE

Because ham radio call signs, once allotted, are, like finger-
prints, an unerring form of identification, the call sign used
in this story has been fudged, to blur any resemblance to
that used by any amateur radio enthusiast.

POACHER'S BAG

CHAPTER I

ANDERSON SAID: "Nothing doing, George. Somebody else can deal with it."

Detective Superintendent George Masters dutifully replied, "Yes, sir," to Anderson and then waited for the Assistant Commissioner (Crime) to offer an explanation for his decision. Masters had been called in for an opinion on a case of g.b.h. which involved—or was thought to involve—a villain with whom he had dealt in the past. Masters naturally thought that after the meeting, the job would automatically come to him. But it appeared he was wrong. Anderson was about to give it to somebody else. Why?

"You know, George, we should work like some of the big firms. Or more like them."

"In what way, sir?"

"More and better man-management. I don't mean the usual fringe benefits which seem to include everything, and I mean everything, from free cars to free schooling for the kids, but paying more attention to each member of the force as an individual. Consulting his or her convenience a little. Respecting, wherever possible, his social and family arrangements. Giving them at least the impression that we care: that we don't like cancelling leave with no warning and pinching rest-days without a blind thought for what domestic havoc it causes."

"I agree, sir, but the exigencies of the service . . ."

"A convenient excuse for perpetrating nonsenses which we can no longer afford, George. I'm not advocating that we turn the force into a squad of nine-to-fivers, merely that we try our utmost to give our people some of the consideration that they have a right to expect nowadays. It is more important than ever, in these days of dwindling manpower, that we let our people see we are trying to treat them like human beings. We fail to attract so many good people and, even worse, lose so many, because we blindly play ducks and drakes with their lives, using the exigencies of the service as an excuse."

Masters waited, wondering what Anderson was leading up to. He suspected that the AC had been asked to write a report along these lines and was trying out his material on him. Or, and here Masters felt a little pang of horror at the thought, the AC was about to ask him, Masters, to write a report as a basis for a senior officers' discussion. That could be why he had told him not to get involved in the g.b.h. case—to leave time for a quick write-up on improved man-management.

"Take Green, for instance," said Anderson. "He's worked with you for a long time. And for most of that time you were at loggerheads with one another." He held up his hand to prevent Masters from interrupting. "I know you agreed to keep him on and even to recommend his promotion a year or so ago, but that doesn't alter the fact that you plagued our lives out at one time with requests for his removal from your team."

Masters bowed his head to acknowledge the accuracy of the comment.

Anderson continued. "I go down to the senior officers' mess every so often. Yesterday I was down there and met Green."

Masters waited. What the hell had Green said to the big man? A complaint? It could be that Anderson, in his present mood, may have been prepared to listen to a verbal beef rather than to demand that the proper channels be used.

"DCI Green was telling me about the vast improvement marriage has wrought in you, George."

Masters stared in amazement.

Anderson grinned. "I don't know that I agree with him on that score, but I do know that I agree with him over his opinion of Mrs Masters. He thinks the world of her, George. And, apparently, so does Mrs Green."

"They get on very well," admitted Masters. "Green looks upon Wanda almost as a daughter and both he and Mrs Green have been very kind."

"That's why it would be unforgivable to rob Green of the weekend with your mother-in-law that he was telling me about. He's looking forward to it so much, George, that if I sent you off on this g.b.h. case and you and he were to miss it, I'd be guilty of a complete disregard of Green's feelings."

"Oh, lord!" groaned Masters.

"Don't tell me you had forgotten that you are going off tomorrow?"

"No, sir. But my mother-in-law is . . . well, Wanda and I are extremely fond of her, but in private we refer to her as the Great Dictator. I don't think she and Green will get along all that well, so I had hoped he wasn't setting too much store by the visit."

" I see. But why did you invite him?"

"I didn't. Mrs Bartholomew did. Wanda has talked of Green in her presence and so the *diktat* was issued. Bring Green! I had no idea he was looking forward to it quite so much. In fact, I was pretty sure he only accepted to please Wanda when she invited him, and that he would be glad of an excuse to cry off."

Anderson shook his head. "Far from it, George. Make sure you get off tomorrow in good time. Somebody else will look after the g.b.h. case. Probably Rowe. He seems to be the least busy of the likely candidates. I'll pass your opinion on to him. And have a good time in . . . where is it?"

"In Wiltshire, sir. Winterbourne Cardinal, actually."

They were using the Masters' own car. Before their marriage, Wanda and George had both owned cars. Now they had disposed of these and splurged on just one. An XJ6.

They picked up the Greens at a few minutes before two on the Friday afternoon. Wanda was driving. Knowing that Green hated car travel, but was least uneasy if allowed to occupy the nearside rear seat, Masters suggested that Mrs Green should take the front passenger seat while he sat alongside the DCI in the back.

They took the pretty route, avoiding the motorway. It was a fine, mid-October afternoon, with a bright sun to illuminate the autumn colours and with just a faint nip in the air to crisp everything up and to make one think of open fires, comfortable armchairs and— come four o'clock—toasted muffins dripping in butter.

"Wanda's mother . . ." began Green.

9

"You'll like her," said Masters.

"I do like her," retorted Green.

"But how . . .?"

"I met her at your wedding. We had quite a chat."

"Of course. I had forgotten. She left a good impression, did she?"

"I must confess I was afraid she wouldn't. She's a bit self-willed, if you'll pardon me mentioning it."

"Don't apologise," said Wanda. "George and I call her the Great Dictator."

Mrs Green laughed. "I'm not sure you should have told us that. It will stick in our minds and we shall give ourselves away every time she is the least bit imperious."

"Not it," said Masters. "But I'd be interested to hear what caused your husband to like her, despite her manner."

"She has standards," said Green. "I was arguing with her . . ."

"You were what?"

"Over the champagne," said Mrs Green. "They'd both had several glasses by that time."

"Rubbish," said Green. "A few glasses of kali-water don't affect me, and you know it, Doris."

"The subject of the argument?" demanded Masters.

"None of your business," replied Green. "Strictly private."

"I see. At any rate Bella must have been impressed with your argument."

"Bella?" asked Mrs Green. "Please tell me, George. Is that what we are to call her?"

"Wanda and I always do. She answers to it."

Masters kept the idle conversation going, thinking to take Green's mind off the journey. He seemed to succeed, though for a time he wondered whether the DCI—being as chauvinistic a male pig as anybody Masters had ever met—might not object to a woman driver. But Green seemed happy enough and was even able to help Wanda, who lost her way in the one-way system in Salisbury, to find the Amesbury Road which she knew so well.

"Winterbourne Cardinal," said Green, "is a new one on me. There's lots of Winterbournes round here. I was stationed in

Winterbourne Gunner and Winterbourne Dauntsey very early on in the last struggle."

"It'll be home ground for you then," said Masters.

"It's a long time ago." Green started to reminisce, as he always did when offered the chance. "We used to get a bus from the camps into Salisbury in those days. That's when bus companies offered a service. Right from the guard room to the middle of Salisbury for threepence. Fivepence if you took a return. But to get anywhere else, off the bus route, was a bit difficult. Of course, army trucks used to run about and you could often thumb a lift to get somewhere, but as often as not, if you wanted to go out in the evenings to somewhere besides Salisbury, you had to walk."

"It's very open country," said Wanda, "with miles of empty road between villages."

"I remember," said Green. "But what of it? We were young and fit and we hadn't been used to motor cars, so we didn't miss them. But I'll tell you about one place we found once. I never knew its name. We were only interested in its pub, if you follow me, but the funny thing is that over the years, I've thought about that place often."

"You'd like to go back there?"

"I'd love to. It was a nice place. Pretty. Though at the time we'd have gone back for a different reason."

"Oh yes? Why?"

"Because the landlord sold us bad beer and it made us sick. It was the summer of nineteen forty. Very hot and the beer short. So I reckon that bloke sold us squaddies some beer that was off. Three of us. We had one pint apiece, and how we got home on our flat feet I'll never know."

"It's perhaps just as well you didn't know where it was or what it was called, otherwise you might have done the landlord a mischief."

"First off, yes. But later, no. As I told you, it was a pretty little place."

"What was it you remember about it?" asked his wife.

"I must have told you. It was off the main road. Not very big. The main thing was the village pond and this pub like a Canadian log cabin just alongside it. Only it wasn't a log cabin, of course. But it was wood. Tarred outside. And thatched."

"Go on," said Masters quietly.

"I was told it was a very old barn."

"You're quite right," said Masters. "It was."

"How do you know?"

"Because you have just given us a rough word-picture of the pub at Winterbourne Cardinal. It's known as the Cardinal Grange . . ."

"Grange? That's a funny name for a public house. For a private house, perhaps . . . but for a pub!"

"The Grange is believed to be one of the very few remaining examples of the transition between Saxon and early Tudor timber buildings. It was one of the granges—which in this sense means grain store or barn—of the Priory which in turn was an offshoot of a pre-Cistercian Abbey founded by King Stephen. The Abbey has disappeared, and nobody knows exactly where it was, though there is a strong body of opinion that it was somewhere over Old Sarum way."

"It all sounds very interesting," said Doris Green. "Especially as it is William's lost village from so many years back."

"Quite."

"What I want to know," said Green, "is where the Cardinal comes in? Abbots and Priors would seem to be right. But a Cardinal, no."

"The origins of the name are lost in history, too," said Masters. "For my part, I think some Prince of the Church—in the days when they weren't above such things—thought he'd like a stake in real estate and annexed the village for himself."

"From his own people?"

"For a senior detective, you are quite naïve, Bill," said Wanda, gently, giving Green no cause for offence. "The abbeys and priories waxed fat in those days. They were very wealthy, when in fact they should have been quite poor institutions. So when one of the big boys of the church took a fancy to a bit of their property, he could chastise the abbots and priors for laying up for themselves treasure on earth, and then promptly take what he wanted for himself."

"Daylight robbery, you mean?"

"With no nice Mr Green from Scotland Yard to put things right. Just so. And here's the turning.",

"Bella will tell you," said Masters, "that the village got its name because the cardinal flower grows here in great profusion."

"I don't think I know it," said Mrs Green.

"Red lobelia. The same red as the cardinal's hat. It's a feature of the village in spring and summer."

"Village ahead," said Wanda, turning left-handed on to an even more minor road. "Your memory come to life, Bill."

Green leaned forward. "That's it. I can see the pond. And the pub. Yes. It's still got that railing outside."

"What railing?" asked his wife.

"That white post and rail fence. The one I leant over to be sick."

Wanda's mother, Bella Bartholomew, had natural, grey, elaborately coiffeured hair. Her face was long, but relatively unlined, and although she was in her middle fifties, her skin had none of the parchment-like quality which the prolonged and heavy use of cosmetics so often causes. Her dress had the elegance of simplicity. It was of navy blue moygashel with a relieving white belt. Her shoes were of classic court style to match, the medium heel showing off to advantage as taut and shapely a pair of legs as ever wore 15-denier nylons. Her only jewellery was a small string of white beads, a gold watch and her two rings. Her hands, very slender, showed little of the ageing process that is so often the give-away when mutton tries to disguise itself as lamb. The nails, carefully manicured and shaped, were enhanced by nothing more than a colourless varnish. The voice was incisive or, as had been hinted earlier, even imperious, but seemed never to bray the inanities of the idle-minded. Ever since he had first met her, she had reminded Masters of the principal of a women's college in a major university, so authoritative was her manner.

She was waiting for them at her door as the car drew up. She greeted them individually, and Green was careful not to smile at the—to him—amusing sight of Masters being kissed by his mother-in-law. But something of his amusement must have got through to his hostess who, instead of ignoring it, chose to imply that she had misread it as amazement.

"Mr Green, you are surprised to find that my front door opens straight from the pavement. Did you envisage me as hidden away behind acres of lawns, with an impressive drive and a pillared portico?"

"I don't know what I expected, ma'am . . ."

She interrupted him. "Before we go any further, could I invite you to call me Bella? Or Isobel if you prefer not to shorten it. I fully intend to call you William, and I trust Mrs Green will not consider it unduly familiar if I address her as Doris."

"You know my name?" asked Mrs Green.

"The wise hostess does her homework, Doris. But come in all of you. George, why not leave the bags until you put the car in?"

"I'll do that now." He turned to Wanda. "You have the keys. If we could open the boot . . ."

Mrs Bartholomew ushered the Greens indoors, and then Green did whistle with amazement.

"William!" admonished his wife, scandalised.

"Well, just look at it." He gestured with his arm. "Bella was asking me if I was surprised that her door opened straight off the pavement like a back-to-back in 'Coronation Street'. And I would have been, if it hadn't been a great double-leaf affair in heavy oak, studded with iron and set in a pointed arch. But now this hall. Look at it. Twenty foot each way if it's an inch. Oak beams, a fire, a floor you could see your face in and rugs, to say nothing of those little wrought-iron wall-lights . . ."

"It's rude to comment, William."

"Not if it's done appreciatively," said Bella. "I'm very lucky to have so beautiful a house. It is the last remaining property of the old Priory. Not the main building, of course, but one of its guest houses and stores. The bits that have been added on since have allowed successive occupants to turn this, which was once the main room, into the hall. As you can see, the staircase, though old, is relatively modern compared with the original stud work. At one time, I imagine, there was nothing more than a simple ladder leading to the upper floor. I believe it led from what is now my dining room."

"It's really beautiful," said Doris Green, "and you keep it so beautiful."

"Not I. Ena. Ena Cully. She has been with me since shortly after my marriage. I confess that without Ena I should be lost. She is a benevolent, tireless worker of my own age, and we two have come to rely upon each other more and more as the years have gone by." She finished quite simply: "We are good companions."

By this time Masters and Wanda had the bags in the hall and the car parked in the garage entrance beside the house.

"We are ready for tea?"

"Go ahead," said Masters. "I'll take the cases upstairs."

"Very well, but don't be long. I particularly want you to be present."

Masters looked across at Bella. "That sounds as though there is something of importance you wish to say."

"There is, so please be quick, George."

"Bella," said Wanda, "whatever it is can wait for a minute or two. You haven't even given William and Doris time to freshen up . . ."

Mrs Bartholomew raised her well-kept hands in horror at her own forgetfulness. "How very remiss of me. Wanda, while George takes the bags up, show Doris and William into the back room. You and George will have to be in the front this time." She turned to Doris. "I know the back room sounds ghastly, but it is, in fact, the room over the study and it overlooks the garden. It is far quieter than the front room which is immediately over our heads and gets all the street noise."

"If there is any," suggested Green.

"Oh, there is, at weekends. There is a public house which gets very busy on Saturdays. Apart from the vocal jollity this engenders, a great many of the patrons seem to be possessed of high-powered motor cycles, the engines of which rend the night air to a point where I would not be surprised were I to wake up one morning to find one of these modern black holes hovering above the village. That is, of course, if black holes can hover."

Green, a little uncomfortable at the idea of Masters carrying his bag, picked it up and made for the stairs. Finding himself alone with the Superintendent, he asked: "What's it all about?

If she wants to talk to you all that particularly, Doris and I had better hang back a bit until it's over."

Masters shook his head as he led the way round the bend in the stairs. "I haven't any idea what she's on about, but it won't be private, otherwise she'd have arranged to get me on my own. Besides, as far as I know, there's literally nothing . . . what I mean is, if there's some family business to discuss she's more likely to make a confidante of Wanda than she is of me. What you've got to remember is that I don't know the old dear all that well myself."

"I suppose not." They stopped outside a door. "Is this it?"

"That's it. We're directly opposite. Bella has the main room—that's to the left of the stairhead—while Ena Cully has the room beyond us, opposite the bathroom which is, incidentally, next door to you."

Green nodded his thanks for the information and entered his room, leaving the door open for Doris to follow after she, in turn, had been given a brief picture of the layout from Wanda.

"Toast," said Bella. "In the chafing dish, William. Hand it to Doris, would you?"

Green said: "I won't show my ignorance by pretending I don't know what a chafing dish is, but I've never come across one before. Not to have someone tell me my toast is in it, that is. We usually use a rack."

"It's in the dish because it's ready buttered."

Green lifted the heavy lid and passed the big oval silver dish to his wife. "False bottom, I suppose?"

"That's right. I believe one could use charcoal in them, and such was done at one time. But Ena Cully and I prefer boiling water. It's far cleaner and altogether more convenient. Where we don't mind boiling kettles, we would dislike having to ignite and fan coals into life."

Tea was well under way before Bella broached the subject she had earlier seemed so anxious to discuss.

"I moved here," she said, "when Wanda married the first time. Two of the people who became my friends were Jennifer and Haydn Prior." She turned to her daughter. "You met them once or twice, I believe, on your visits here?"

"Yes. I liked them. Mr Prior was, I believe, an academic who designed something and made a fair bit of money out of it, wasn't he?"

Mrs Bartholomew picked up the silver teapot. "He designed a number of small items. Nothing spectacular in the lay-world, like the man who made a million from designing a work-bench. But in certain industrial areas he was able to perfect or speed up processes which saved a great deal of money, and his reputation grew to such an extent that he was often called in as a consultant. He always said of himself, somewhat disparagingly, that he was a bottle-neck remover."

"I hadn't realised quite what a useful man he must be," said Wanda. "But his wife died, didn't she?"

"Almost four years ago."

Masters put down his cup. "May I ask why you are telling us all this, Bella?"

"Certainly you may. A few months ago, in early July, to be precise, Haydn Prior asked me to marry him."

"Good for him," said Masters. "His choice does him credit. Did you accept him?"

"Yes."

"Why didn't you tell us?" asked Wanda.

"Wanted to keep it quiet, perhaps," said Green. "I know I would. There's something a bit private about an arrangement like that. Something you want to keep to yourself and . . . what's the word? . . . savour, alone."

"Quite right, William. When one is no longer young enough for orange blossom, it is better to make no fuss."

"When's the wedding?" asked Mrs Green. "And where are you going to live?"

"I shall continue to live here."

"You will?" asked Masters. "What about your husband? Don't tell me you are going to keep up separate houses after your marriage?"

"There isn't going to be a marriage."

"Isn't . . .?" Wanda stopped after the one word and there was a short uncomfortable silence.

"Thought better of it, have you?" asked Green eventually.

"Perhaps it's just as well you told us, because I was about to congratulate you."

"I didn't think better of it, William. That is, I didn't change my mind about marrying Haydn."

"Oh, dear," said Wanda. "He hasn't jilted you, has he?"

Bella shook her head. "He's dead."

"Dead? Mr Prior? When did he die?"

"Just over three weeks ago. We were to have been married tomorrow. That is why I invited you all for this weekend."

"As your side of the family, you mean?" asked Doris Green. "That was very sweet of you."

Bella inclined her head gracefully. Masters said quietly: "I'm terribly sorry about what you've just told us. But I can't help feeling that when you insisted on this teatime discussion you had something to tell us more momentous even than what we've just heard. How did Mr Prior die?"

His mother-in-law looked across at him and said without emotion: "He was murdered."

Again there was an appreciable silence. The sitting room was one of the later additions to the house. Situated to the left of the old hall, it was Georgian built. In classic proportions, it was long, running from the front to the back of the house, with a window in each end. These were covered in burgundy tapestry curtains which fell in great folds to the floor. Their richness in the firelight was enhanced by the shadows in the folds. The two or three pieces of furniture scattered round the walls—a desk, chiffonier and corner cupboard—were of mahogany, but lightly made, with none of the depressing heaviness that the material has inspired in so many pieces. The armchairs were generous, newly covered in glazed chintz which showed off the blue of Canterbury bells against the green of maidenhair fern on a cream background. It was peaceful: at peace with the world. And now—murder!

"No!" said Masters quietly. "No! Not with Wanda here."

They all understood him well enough. A little over two years ago, Wanda had been drawn into a murder case. Innocent though she had been of all complicity, it had taken a deal of hard work on the part of Masters and Green to free her completely. Now her mother had announced that Prior had been murdered. It was too close to home for Masters who feared on Wanda's behalf.

Wanda, her long fair hair glinting in the firelight moved quickly across to her mother and knelt at her knee, taking her hands as she did so. "Mummy, are you sure?"

Her mother freed a hand to stroke her hair. "Certain, my dear. Positively certain."

"Do the police think so?" asked Green.

"Oh, yes, William. In fact they have charged a man."

"With Mr Prior's murder?"

"Yes."

"How did he die?" asked Masters.

"He was shot—with a shotgun—and in making his escape, suffered a heart attack due, no doubt, to the frenzied effort he made to get away from his pursuer."

"Let me get this clear," said Masters. "A man shot Mr Prior and wounded him. Prior then made off and the man followed him. Presumably to fire at him again. But before that happened, Prior had a heart attack and died?"

"That is the police theory."

"Theory be blowed," expostulated Green. "If you fire a weapon and wound a man and the victim, in trying to escape— vigorously—suffers a heart attack and dies, that is murder. The one has directly caused the death of the other. Encompassed it, if you want to be technical."

"Appearances can be deceptive."

"I don't see that. The shotgun wounded Mr Prior?"

"Indeed. He was peppered with shot and there was a great deal of blood about his face, I understand. But the wounds were superficial. I am not awfully well informed about shotguns, but this was not a twelve-bore. It was a small four-ten."

"That doesn't matter in the slightest," said Masters. "A gunshot wound, whether slight or severe, will alarm the victim. He will take vigorous action to avoid further violence. If, as a result of that enforced action the wounded victim dies, the crime is that of murder. The man's counsel may plead accidental discharge— which would or could cause equal alarm in the patient and thus result in his death—and on these grounds may ask for the charge to be reduced to that of manslaughter or for it to be thrown out altogether. But that is a decision for the lawyers and the courts to take. Not policemen."

Bella Bartholomew regarded her son-in-law severely. "I am well aware of what you have just said, George."

"I'm sure you are. So I can't help wondering why we are having this particular discussion."

"Because the police have arrested and charged the wrong man."

"How can you possibly make that out? Unless you know that there were two armed men on the scene."

"Only one. Our local poacher, Sid Lunn. He was seen kneeling beside the body, with his hand inside the jacket."

"He denies he shot Prior?"

"No. He admits that, but claims that Haydn's sudden appearance in the spinney where he—Lunn, that is—was after rabbits, caused him to press his trigger involuntarily."

"You obviously believe Lunn's story, but the police do not. Is that it?"

"Precisely."

"It won't wash, old dear," said Green familiarly. "If the shot was unintentional, why did Lunn chase Prior and try to rob the body?"

"He ran after him to see if he needed help."

"Go on," said Masters. "You're interesting me."

"Am I, George?"

"I've been wondering why, had he intended to kill Prior, Lunn had not fired again. Presumably the two were close enough to each other during the get-away for a second shot to have been effective?"

"How long was the chase?" asked Green.

"For its exact length, you would need to measure for yourselves. But my estimate is well over a hundred yards."

"Through or over what sort of country?"

"Very difficult underfoot. The first forty or so yards within the spinney itself. Then came sixty or seventy yards over rough grass down the edge of the spinney, through a five-barred gate and finally along twenty or thirty yards of road."

Masters grimaced thoughtfully.

"Don't make faces, George. If you have something distasteful

20

or contradictory to say, please say it and don't imply it by means of facial gestures."

"Mother," said Wanda firmly, "you are becoming insufferable. If you intend to continue this discussion, please adopt a more conciliatory tone."

Masters laid a hand on one of Wanda's. "Save it, poppet. Bella is obviously incensed over what she regards as police injustice or stupidity. It takes people that way, sometimes. And as Bill and I are not prepared to take her word for it that our local colleagues are at fault, preferring to make our own judgement on what we can elicit from her, she is becoming a little impatient. Thinks us dense or dilatory, she does. But we ain't."

"In my day," said Bella, "the answer to that pretty speech would have been, 'balderdash'. Now, I believe the retort would have been even shorter though initially identical."

Masters grinned. "For that remark, if for no other reason, you can be sure of our full attention. So, what I was about to ask when you let off your broadside was this."

"Yes?"

"At what time was Mr Prior shot?"

"At two a.m. on a moonlight night."

"By a skilled poacher, you said?"

"Highly skilled. With years of undetected crime to his credit. Or do I mean debit?"

"Either will do." Masters looked across at Green. "How's your knowledge of poachers? Mine is small, but I understand that they have eyes like owls . . ."

"Owls? Hawks, you mean."

"Owls. They see in the dark."

"Got you."

"They are quick, silent movers."

"Like jaguars," said Doris. "Or do I mean cheetahs?"

"Again, either will do admirably," replied Masters. "So we have a man who can see well and run lithely, even in the dark, accustomed to working among trees and in open country, following—if not chasing—a man rising sixty who, we are told, was originally an academic and latterly an industrial inventor. Neither of those two pursuits would equip him well for movement cross-country at night and his age would be an overwhelming handicap in such a contest." He turned to Bella. "Can you tell us at what range the initial shot was fired?"

"At not more than twelve yards, according to the experts who can tell these things."

"Forensic?" asked Green. "How do you know that?"

"Haydn's solicitor told me. Not the police."

"Why should he tell you this?"

"He came to see me, naturally, because Haydn had informed him of his forthcoming marriage to me."

"There was to be a new will and settlements and that sort of thing?"

"Quite what provisions Haydn was making, I am not sure. But I understand that I figured largely in whatever he was proposing."

"As his wife, that would be right. But his death will have changed things a bit, won't it?"

"Completely. The new will was drafted but not signed. That, however, is immaterial. His previous testament stands. Haydn had no family, so his entire estate goes to a number of foundations and societies in which he was interested."

"Bad luck."

"I am content, William. I have enough for my needs."

"Lucky, then."

"Yes, I think so. But to get back to George's question. Haydn's solicitor came to see me as a matter of courtesy to let me know how matters stood concerning the estate. Naturally he told me what he knew of his . . . his client's death. The police had given him as full an account as they could of the circumstances. One of the facts was that Haydn had been shot at a range of something less than twelve yards." She turned to Masters. "Am I giving you enough pertinent information to help you come to a conclusion?"

"You're helping wonderfully. But don't be prickly. We're not out to thwart you." He turned again to Green, who said: "I agree with the point you're making, George. With only a twelve yard start in the dark in undergrowth, an elderly man would stand no earthly against a much younger, skilled poacher. This Sid

Lunn could have caught up with Prior and pumped another cartridge load of pellets into him at any time if he'd wanted to.'

"So we can assume he didn't wish to shoot him down?"

Green nodded.

"Wait, wait!" said Wanda. "Couldn't Sid Lunn have lost Mr Prior in the dark or among the trees?"

"A very good question, honeybun," said Green, beaming at Wanda. "But one your old man wouldn't have asked."

"Why not?"

"Because he's already covered it. It was a moonlight night, and in any case Lunn had cat's eyes. He could see in the dark. And he'd be able to hear well, too. Prior would crash about when he was running through the trees. No hope of avoiding a skilled poacher."

"I see. What if Mr Prior hid?"

"Then Lunn would know, because there'd be no noise. And hiding twelve yards away from a poacher who'd already seen you would be like me trying to hide from a strafing Messerschmitt behind a bit of scrub six inches high in the middle of the desert."

"Did you really do that, Bill?" asked his wife.

"Scores of times. I knew it was useless, but you'd be surprised how much confidence it gave me."

"There we are then," said Masters. "We're all satisfied that Lunn didn't wish to gun Prior down. Yet he followed him. If, as we've been told, it was to see if Prior needed help, why didn't Lunn catch up and ask if help was needed or to see for himself how badly Prior was wounded?"

"That's a weakness in his story," admitted Green. "I'd have expected somebody like Lunn who is, after all, nothing more nor less than a tea-leaf, to have made off in the opposite direction if he'd meant Prior no more harm."

"Are you speaking from experience, William?" demanded Bella.

"Long years of it."

"Of tea-leaves? I think that was your term?"

Green nodded.

"But not of poachers?"

"No. I've never nicked one so far as I can remember."

"And if he can't remember," said Masters, "he hasn't."

Bella Bartholomew turned to Green. "William, I must confess that my knowledge of poachers is not great. But I do know Sid Lunn."

"You know him?"

"I am well acquainted with him. His profession is not that of poacher, you know. That is merely a side-line. A profitable hobby which earns a return no tax man can milk. Sid feeds his own family—and others—on food that would otherwise never be used. I can only applaud that and admire his ability to do so. I wish I could almost manage to feed this household at no cost either to myself or others."

"Or others?" asked Green. "There's an old saying. No lunches are free. He's pinching food that rightly belongs to others."

"It may rightly belong, but it is never used. Sid Lunn would never poach game that is being reared. Not pheasant or partridge. He takes hare and rabbit, with pigeon in season, from areas that are not normally shot over. Far from robbing the rightful owners, he could be said to be doing the owners a great service and saving them a deal of money. Have you any idea how much crop damage is done by rabbits, hares and pigeons, William?"

"I've heard it said that, nationwide, it runs into millions."

"Many millions."

"That's all very well," countered Green, "but do the local landowners and farmers see it in that light?"

Bella smiled.

"Why else do you suppose Sid Lunn has never been caught? Oh, I know he's good at the game, but even the best would be no match for the opposition if there were many determined to catch him."

"Fair enough, Bella," said Green. "So Sid Lunn is a different breed of tea-leaf from the sort I usually meet. So what?"

"My point is just this. I honestly believe that Sid Lunn would have been concerned for Haydn. But he could not possibly have known how seriously Haydn had been hurt. Lunn is canny. He would not wish to give himself away if the wound were only trifling, and, as he could see Haydn was quite capable of making a get-away, all the indications must have been that such was the case. So, my belief is that Sid Lunn hung back, but kept

Haydn in view, lest the need for help arose. If it should not arise, Lunn would be able to slink away to safety."

"He would have been suspected if Prior had mentioned the incident to the police."

"Maybe. But Lunn is not our only poacher, you know, and even the police cannot proceed without evidence. And it is also my belief that our local police would be slow to suspect Lunn of shooting a fellow human being. He may be a poacher, but he is not a man of violence and, as I have hinted earlier, should a local family ever be in need of a good meal, Lunn's spoils would be left on their kitchen table. The recipients would know where the food had come from, but the benefactor would expect neither payment nor thanks."

"What you are saying, Bella, is that this poacher would not injure Mr Prior, so the police have arrested the wrong man?" asked Mrs Green.

"Not quite. I told you that Lunn had been seen by our local constable, Rowe, with his hand inside Haydn's jacket. The police have interpreted that to mean that Lunn was about to rob the body. Haydn, incidentally, was carrying a wallet containing thirty-two pounds in his inside pocket."

"Undisturbed?" asked Masters.

"Undisturbed and intact. Lunn claims to have been feeling Haydn's heart to see if he could detect life."

"That sounds reasonable, whether it is the truth or not."

"Thank you, George. If you can prove it is not the truth, then I shall accept your word."

"If I can prove it?"

"You and William?"

"Just a moment, Bella. This case is not ours. We cannot interfere."

"You are senior policemen. Detectives."

"So we are. But that fact gives us no authority outside the Metropolitan area unless we are specifically invited to participate in some investigation. The local police here have treated Prior's death as a murder case and they have the suspect under lock and key, committed for trial. They have no reason to call us in, but they would have every reason to object strongly if either William or myself as much as murmured the slightest intention of interesting ourselves in their business."

"That is rubbish, George. They have arrested the wrong man. This is still England—just. But that final word—just—must always apply. And just because the bureaucrats draw demarcation lines it does not mean that justice shall not be done."

"Justice will be done—in the courts."

"You call subjecting an innocent man to the business of a murder trial, justice? That is law, not justice."

"Sorry, Bella, there is nothing we can do."

Wanda said, "They would like to help. I'm sure they would. But you haven't even given them cause for . . ."

"For what?"

"Interesting themselves. By that, I mean for approaching anybody, even unofficially. You insist Mr Prior was murdered, yet you are equally adamant that the only other person on the scene—a man who confesses to having wounded him—did not commit the murder. George and William may respect your feelings, intuition, or whatever you like to call it, but those feelings are not grounds for making an official approach to anybody."

"There is nobody I could possibly approach either officially or unofficially," said Masters, "except one man. And it is doubtful whether he could tell me anything."

"Who is this one man?" asked Doris Green.

"You haven't been listening, love," said her husband. "The only one non-official source open to us would be Mr Prior's solicitor. And we couldn't go to him and suggest that Scotland Yard had any interest whatsoever. George might just speak to him as Bella's son-in-law. As though he was having a word just by way of looking after her interests. Unofficially."

Bella looked across at Masters. "Is that right, George?"

Masters nodded. "But don't imagine he will be in sympathy with you. He's not likely to be well-disposed towards a man he considers has murdered a valuable client."

Doris Green asked: "What exactly are you asking these men to do, Bella? Or, rather, what do you hope to achieve by trying to get them to interfere?"

"I believe that the wrong man is being indicted for the murder.

26

I would like to see that put right on two counts. First, I feel that in the interests of justice the real murderer should stand in the dock and, second, as the most intimately bereaved by Haydn's death, I have a great personal desire to make the real killer pay the penalty for his crime."

"Understandable," grunted Green. "But you're asking us to do the impossible, based on nothing more than a gut feeling."

"I will not be beaten," said Bella. "I shall ring Geoffrey Pulker immediately."

"Pulker being Prior's solicitor, I suppose?"

"Quite right."

"With what excuse?"

"I shall ask him for sherry tomorrow morning. He knows of you, George, and when he visited me, intimated that he would like to meet you sometime."

"How could he know about George?" asked Wanda. "We don't know Mr Pulker . . ."

"When you make a will," explained her mother, "if your man of affairs is any good, he will insist on making provision for all emergencies. Much of Haydn's estate was to have come to me should he die before me; but were I to predecease him—horrid word, predecease—then you would have become a beneficiary. You and George. And, thereafter, any children of your marriage and so on. Haydn had to give Pulker the details."

"I see."

"Now I must ring him. I have his number in my book."

"He won't be in his office now. It's twenty to seven."

"So it is. Why don't you people all get ready for dinner while I ring his home. George, we will meet again here at half past seven for drinks. I shall have to give Ena Cully a last-minute hand in the kitchen so if I'm a little late, please act as host."

Wanda and Doris had elected to carry the tea tray into the kitchen to help Ena Cully and to give Mrs Green a chance to meet her. As the two men went upstairs, Masters said: "Get down again as soon as you can, Bill. I want a private word. And, incidentally, I'd like to apologise for this business. I had no idea I'd be bringing you on a busman's holiday."

"Forget it. It's not your fault. And the old lady's a cracker. If it amuses her . . ."

"She's in deadly earnest."

"Maybe," said Green. "When I play dominoes in a pub I'm in deadly earnest, but it's still only a game."

"Thanks for taking it that way. I hope Doris won't mind too much."

"Mind? She's in her element. This house and Bella! And you know what she thinks of Wanda. Just being here's enough to keep her more than happy."

"I'm glad to hear it. See you shortly."

When the two men met at about ten past seven, Masters poured drinks and the two of them stood, backs to the fire.

"Cheers!"

"Cheers. Look here, Greeny, has the same question occurred to you as to me—leaving aside Bella's whimsy about a phantom murderer?"

"Of course it has. But I didn't like to ask Bella why a man of nearly sixty was cavorting round the countryside at two in the morning in September."

"Without a coat."

"Right. Was he crackers?"

"I never met him. But if Bella had agreed to marry him, I'd have sworn he couldn't have been. I mean, she's not the sort to suffer fools gladly, let alone marry one."

"Don't get me wrong—but not even for the lolly?"

Masters shook his head. "She's fairly comfortable as she is. I can't see her teaming up with a nutcase no matter how rich."

"I'll take your word for it, because I reckon the same thing myself. But there's crackers and crackers. Prior may not have been a loony, but he was a professor and an inventor, both of whom are popularly reckoned to be a bit forgetful if not actually round the bend."

"True. Here, let me get you a refill." Green drained his glass and handed it over. Masters went across to the corner wine cupboard. "Could he have heard Sid Lunn and gone to see what was going on?"

"That depends. Ta!" said Green accepting his drink. "How close to his house was the spinney?"

"Perhaps even more important, was it his spinney? If so, he might have been interested if he thought a poacher was there. If it wasn't his land, why bother?"

Green put his glass on the mantelpiece behind him. "I'm sorry to harp on about the state of Prior's mind, George, but when she was telling us what happened, Bella said—and I quote—that his sudden appearance in the spinney caused Lunn to press the trigger involuntarily. Now I'm no countryman. But if Lunn was as good a poacher as we've been led to believe, he'd have heard Prior coming a mile away."

"Agreed."

"But he didn't. So we've got to suppose Prior was in the wood before Lunn arrived."

"Yes."

"So that knocks on the head any theory about Prior going to see what Lunn was up to."

"Go on."

"And it also means that Prior was lying low. At any rate Lunn didn't know he was there, otherwise his sudden appearance wouldn't have frightened him."

"Good."

"And then, the sudden appearance itself. What does that mean, George?"

"Heaven knows."

"When Lunn is twelve yards away, Prior suddenly appears. Quick enough to cause Lunn to fire involuntarily. That sounds to me almost as though Prior jumped out on him. No, not on him, exactly, but in front of him. In a scary sort of way. And any chap who jumps out in front of an armed man in the middle of a wood at night is crackers. Not in full possession of his faculties—or not enough to appreciate the danger of doing so."

Masters nodded. "Thanks, Greeny. I'm beginning to think Sid Lunn has been wrongly charged, but not for the reasons Bella gives."

Before Green could comment, the door opened and Wanda ushered Doris in. "There you are, you see. They sneaked down here without us to get a quick one in without our knowing."

"We're two up on you actually," said Masters. "Now what's it to be? Sherry?"

It was twenty to eight before Bella appeared. Like the other two women, she had changed into a long skirt. "I'll have a dry Martini, please, George. Two to one. Not too big, because we haven't much time."

"What's the hurry?" asked Wanda as her husband prepared the drink. "Something spoiling in the kitchen?"

"No," said Bella, seating herself very elegantly. "We are having a guest after dinner."

"Oh? Who?"

"Mr Pulker. He's driving over from Salisbury to take coffee with us."

"But you said you were inviting him for sherry tomorrow morning."

"That is what I did. But he asked if he could call this evening."

"For any particular reason?" asked Masters, handing her the drink.

She popped the olive into her mouth before replying. Then she said: "Oh yes. He was quite excited, poor man."

"Why?"

"He told me there had been an important new development which he thought I ought to know about immediately."

CHAPTER II

By FIVE MINUTES to nine they had finished dinner and Green
was still singing the praises of a lemon *soufflé* which, he said, was
the best pud he'd had in years because it ate like pud, looked like
pud and tasted like pud and yet had the lightness of an ethereal
being.

"Why ethereal?" asked Masters as Wanda got to her feet to
remove the last of the dishes to the kitchen.

"Because," replied Green, "I know I'm full, but I don't feel it."

"Not bloated, you mean?"

"If you like. But I knew before I had it I didn't want it because I'd made a pig of myself with the first course and . . ."

"Bill!" His wife sounded scandalised.

"He asked."

"Quite right," said Masters. "I feel the same myself. I just
wondered why William chose the adjective ethereal."

"Isn't he right?"

"He's so right it isn't true. How do modern physicists regard
the ether? As a subtle substance which permeates all space. That's
what the *soufflé* is and has done. Subtly filled all spaces without
bloating." He turned to Bella. "We're singing its praises."

"Tell Ena Cully. She cooked it. Now, I think we should move
to the sitting room. We'll have coffee there when Pulker arrives,
which he should do at any minute." She got to her feet. "George,
I only have brandy and Benedictine by way of liqueurs, so don't
be offering a free selection."

Masters opened the door and the three women passed through,
but Green held back.

"I want a quick fag before I go in there."

"Bella doesn't mind if we smoke in the sitting room."

31

"I know. But she'll expect us to wait for coffee."

"Humbug, Greeny. Yes, I'll pinch one of your fags just to keep you company, but what's the real reason for hanging back?"

"I'm not criticising, George . . ."

"Get on with it. If there's something wrong, say so."

"While we were talking about the pudding . . ."

"Yes? I thought you were waffling on for some good reason, but couldn't decide what it could be."

"I saw the dining room door open an inch or so. I was sitting facing it, you know. It stayed open. There was somebody there, listening."

"Somebody? That would be Ena Cully. I'll not insult you by asking if you're sure."

"There's nobody else it could have been?"

"No. If there were, it could appear sinister."

"And you don't think her listening was?"

"The trouble with having a mystery on your hands is that you suspect everything. So of course I find it strange that Ena Cully should listen at the door. But if there were no mystery, I'd just say it was the act of an unobtrusive but efficient housekeeper wanting to know the progress of the meal without interrupting those dining."

Green grunted. "I suppose so. But I don't like listeners at keyholes."

"Neither do I. But you've started something now."

"Sorry, George. But if Bella insists somebody other than the bloke who shot him was getting at Haydn Prior . . . what I mean is, if Bella were to have got married again, what would Ena Cully's position have been?"

Masters looked glum. "The thought had occurred to me. If Bella had gone to live in Prior's house where, presumably, there is already a housekeeper, Ena Cully would be out on her ear. And to prevent that, she might not have wanted the marriage to take place. But we don't know any of these facts, Bill. Least of all do we know whom Bella is accusing or what she's accusing them of. After all he did die of a heart attack brought on by vigorous exercise after being wounded. So it's hellish difficult to see what bee she's got in her bonnet."

Green agreed and then added: "But if this Cully woman is implicated, it might explain her listening at doors. She's probably overheard every word that's been said since we arrived."

"That's a point." He stubbed out his cigarette. "Come on, they'll be wondering what we're up to."

Pulker was a man of fifty with a good head of once-dark hair which seemed to be turning grey all-of-a-piece. He was lithe-figured, tall, with a slight bodily stoop which gave an impression of eagerness as he walked. He was wearing a navy blue suit and a tie to match, but despite the severity of his dress, he had a cheerful face and pleasant voice. Bella met him when he rang and ushered him into the sitting room where she immediately went into the lengthy round of introductions.

Coffee followed, Wanda dispensing it. As Masters gave Pulker a brandy balloon, he said: "Mrs Bartholomew has told us something of the circumstances of your client's death. She has also told DCI Green and myself that she is not sure the police are on the right track in charging Lunn with the murder."

"She mentioned something of the sort to me when I called to see her." He turned to his hostess. "You are not trying to involve Scotland Yard in this matter are you, Mrs Bartholomew?"

"Not officially. But I can see no reason why, if I have a senior detective in the family and an equally experienced detective as a friend, I shouldn't voice my doubts to them and, indeed, consult them."

Pulker grinned at her and shook his head slowly. "You're being naughty, my dear lady. May I, as an officer of the court, offer you some advice? These two gentlemen are your guests and—out of courtesy—will listen to what you may have to say. But remember that a policeman is never off duty. You cannot involve a policeman unofficially. They must take official note of all crime, proven or suspected. So you cannot hope to achieve their co-operation without going the whole hog."

"I have expressed my belief that the police have made a mistake. That is the right of every citizen."

"Have you grounds for saying so? Factual grounds rather than just personal beliefs?"

"I believe I have."

"Then you must go to the local police and tell them these facts."

Bella smiled sweetly at him. "Mr Pulker, you have not yet grasped my tactics. Were I to go to the local police, they would, no doubt, listen very politely to what I had to tell them, and then forget it. But if, within the privacy of my own home, I cast my stone into the pool—in other words, if I intrigue George and William enough to cause them to bring their trained minds into play so that they can elicit facts that I may know, but haven't realised I know, then it could be that they—rather than I—may have some cause to question the action of the local police. Should this happen, then—as you have just told us—they would be in duty bound to take some action themselves. In other words, the barrier which prevents them from interfering will have been removed, and I shall have attained my objective."

"You're a devious old so-and-so," said Wanda.

"But very clever," said Doris Green. "Particularly that bit about removing the barrier. And you have got George and Bill interested, Bella, otherwise they wouldn't have gone into a huddle before we came down to dinner and after we left the table."

"All you women are as bad as one another," grumbled Green.

"Am I to understand," asked Pulker, "that you gentlemen have, in fact, deduced some fact or reason for interfering in this case?"

"Not yet," said Masters. "During the huddles Mrs Green referred to, her husband and I have been discussing what we have heard so far. That does not mean that we have unearthed anything that would cause us to approach the local police."

"Nor, apparently, does it mean that you haven't."

"Quite."

"Then you have," cried Bella triumphantly.

"No," said Masters. "All it means is that we have decided that there are a few more questions we should ask you. The answers you give may tip the balance either way or leave us completely undecided. But I understand that Mr Pulker has some urgent information for you. Perhaps we should hear what he has to say—unless it is for your ears only."

Pulker laughed. "Mr Masters, if I said my news was for Mrs Bartholomew only, how long do you think it would be before she recounted it to you?"

"No time at all."

"Exactly. And so, in case what I have to say may affect your decisions, I think it would be better if you were to hear my news first-hand."

"Thank you."

Pulker turned to Bella. "With your permission, Mrs Bartholomew . . ."

She inclined her head. "We are waiting, Mr Pulker."

"When I first called on you, I felt at liberty to disclose that it had been Mr Prior's intention to sign a new will leaving the majority of his estate to you. He would have done this at the time of your marriage. In view of his untimely death, his previous will stands. His estate is to be divided between various institutions in which he had been interested during his lifetime."

"I understood this perfectly, Mr Pulker."

"I am sure you did. Now, however, I have been informed that the will is to be contested."

"By whom? Haydn had no family, no near relations, or so he told me."

"That was his belief, and mine. But now it appears there could be a very close relative indeed."

Bella gazed at him speculatively. "You are being delicate, Mr Pulker. I suspect you are hinting that there is a by-blow in the background."

"A what?" asked Mrs Green.

"A bastard," said her hostess crisply.

"Oh!" Mrs Green sounded slightly shocked. Bella went on: "I don't believe it, Mr Pulker. But no doubt you have good reason for saying so, otherwise you wouldn't be here."

Pulker inclined his head. "A young man, twenty-nine years old, who lives in Paris and is called Harry Gooding, claims that he is the late Mr Prior's natural son by a certain Miss Elsie Gooding."

"Rubbish. What proof does he have?"

"A birth certificate which says that a son was born to a Miss

35

Gooding and fathered by a university lecturer called Haydn Bennet Prior."

"You have seen this certificate?"

"A photostat copy." Pulker took an envelope from his inside pocket. The document he took from it had been folded once, lengthwise. He offered it to Bella. She waved it away. "I'll take your word for what the certificate says. But that won't be proof of what this man Gooding claims."

"I'm pleased to hear you state your scepticism, Mrs Bartholomew. Is your attitude based on any form of fact or simply on your knowledge of the character of your late fiancé?"

"Both."

"Ah!"

"The one great disappointment in Haydn Prior's life was that he had no child. Had he fathered one—particularly a boy—he and his wife would have acknowledged it in some way, so great was their desire to have children. Haydn spoke to me more than once about this, so before I accepted his offer of marriage, I suggested to him that as he was still a virile man, he should marry a woman young enough to have his child. It was then he told me that it was he and not his first wife who was incapable of becoming a parent. In their younger days they had tests done and it was proved conclusively that he was the unproductive partner."

"In that case," asked Masters, "why did they never adopt?"

"His wife refused to consider it."

"Why, if they were both so keen on children?"

"Because she thought the presence of an adopted child would be a constant reproach to Haydn. Had *she* been incapable of bearing a child, then her unsublimated maternal instinct would have carried them through had they adopted. But she was of the opinion that a man who cannot prove his manhood in the generally accepted way has nothing but a sense of frustration and failure and that would militate against a happy adoption. Mrs Prior —presumably to prove her love for her husband—said she would never nurture any child but his. And that is what happened."

"He told you all this?" asked Masters.

"At great length. He was actually looking forward to being

36

a parent to Wanda and, forgive me, to you yourself."

"Some kid!" grunted Green. "So, where does that leave us?"

"I would like to know from Mr Pulker," said Masters, "how Harry Gooding, who lives in Paris, got to know of Prior's death. His murder has not, to the best of my knowledge, been mentioned in the national newspapers. Surely Wanda or myself would have noted something such as a murder in Winterbourne Cardinal even if it had been given only a few column inches in the dailies."

"I myself inserted an announcement in the obituary columns," said Pulker. "Haydn Prior was a well-known man in his various fields. I thought it right to announce simply that he had died suddenly. This fellow Gooding claims to have seen the announcement in the *Daily Telegraph*."

"Claims? Are you doubting that?"

"Shall we say I am taking it with a pinch of salt? I can hardly believe that a young man living in Paris takes one of the leading English newspapers every day and that he then reads the births, marriages and deaths columns. What I should consider even more strange is that he should see such a paper only occasionally and that one of those occasions should be the issue carrying the information that Mr Prior had died. Indeed, I will go so far as to say that if he has actually seen these papers daily and, in addition, has scanned the announcement columns, it has been solely for the purpose of waiting for a Mr Haydn Prior to die, in order to enable him to make a claim upon an estate to which he has no entitlement, but to which his birth certificate may lend a spurious authenticity."

"I got the gist of that," said Green, "and I'm going along with it, at any rate for the moment."

"You have some reservations, Mr Green?"

"Only that I like a bit of proof. What you said is good stuff. But coppers have to prove even good stuff. That's all. I'm not disagreeing."

"Thank you. And you, Mr Masters?"

"I agree with William. We are getting a lot of speculation and very little confirmed fact, so far. I would like just one solid spot of proof."

"The emergence of this claimant is a fact."

"A fact, certainly, but proof of what?"

Pulker shrugged. "Proof that all is not quite as straightforward as I would like it to be."

"To be sure. But you must satisfy yourself as to whether the claim is true or false. Presumably you will ask Gooding to call on you and question him very closely in an effort to arrive at the truth."

"He is coming to see me on Monday."

"You have asked him already?"

"He told me he was coming. In his letter. He is flying to London on Sunday."

"Is he now? That's interesting. By the way, what does that certificate say was his place of birth?"

"The Leicester General Hospital."

"Was Haydn ever in Leicester?" asked Wanda.

"Immaterial, darling," said Masters. "Suppose this is a false claim. Gooding wouldn't have made it without having some answers ready. If Prior was never in Leicester, Gooding will say that his mother went to some area where she was not known for the confinement. It was often done that way. If Haydn was ever in Leicester, that would be a bonus for Gooding. But Gooding's plan would never require that Prior should have lived in Leicester, otherwise finding a victim would become immensely more difficult. But Gooding will know—from *Who's Who* and other sources— Prior's professional movements. He will know the years when he was tutoring at Cambridge or wherever. He will say his mother met his father in Cambridge and went to Leicester for the birth."

Wanda nodded her understanding and then said: "Why did you ask where he was born?"

"If it had been London, I could have rung Sergeant Reed and got him to make a few discreet enquiries. But Leicester is off my patch."

"So you do think there is something to investigate."

Masters grinned at his wife. "Your mother says there is. Mr Pulker says there is. William and I are a bit uneasy. But what are we looking for? What are our objectives? Bella says she wants us to find the real murderer. I don't even understand her request.

Mr Pulker has to satisfy himself as to whether a claim on an estate he is managing is bogus or not. That is a legal affair. Not our pigeon at all. So, I can't help your mother and I can't help Mr Pulker. Not directly, that is."

"Indirectly?"

"As I said, William and I are a little uneasy. For our own satisfaction—and in our own way—we will knock our heads together and see what stars we bring into each other's eyes. But unofficially. No more than that, unless and until we are sure there is some valid reason for interfering."

"I'll go along with that," said Green.

"When will you start your unofficial investigation?" asked Bella.

"Right now," said Green. "George, if there's any beer in the cupboard, I'd rather have that than more brandy."

Masters got to his feet with an apology for not doing his bit as host, while Doris Green scolded her husband for asking for a drink.

"You should wait till you're asked, William."

"I know. But if I'd waited for George I'd have waited till the cows come home. He's spending all his time arguing against interfering, but his mind's full of question marks, not one of which has beer written in front of it."

Wanda laughed. "You mean he's being a bit of a humbug about this. Secretly he's intrigued, and so are you."

"Not quite, love. You're mistaking our motives. We both want to help Bella. And that is the only reason we would consider poking our noses in. George said we are uneasy. What he means is that it's damn difficult to want to help somebody when you shouldn't, particularly if all the signs say there's reason to help but there's no good cause to. And if you can sort that little lot out, you're welcome."

Masters handed Green his beer and Pulker—the only other taker—another brandy. Green took a long swig from his glass and then turned to Bella. "Ready?" he asked.

She inclined her head. "Ready, William."

"Right. Tell me why a sober-minded citizen rising sixty should have been cavorting in a spinney at two o'clock of an early autumn morning."

Bella regarded him for a moment. "I wondered when you two would get round to asking that."

Pulker said: "It never occurred to me to wonder why Haydn Prior was out at that time in the morning."

"Not just out," said Green. "Anybody can be out until two. But there has to be some reason why a man is hiding in a wood at that time."

"Could it not be that he heard the poacher and went to investigate?"

"No," said Green emphatically. "That is one of the possibilities George and I have already disposed of—when we were hobnobbing earlier."

"You're quite right," admitted Bella.

"The reason, love," demanded Green.

"This is so difficult," said his hostess.

"From the beginning," prompted Green.

Bella sat silent for a moment or two and then began. "The point is that during the last week or so of his life, Haydn was strange."

"How, strange?" asked Wanda.

"Leave this to me, sweetie," said Green. He turned back to Bella. "Not to put too fine a point on it, he went crackers, didn't he?"

"Billy! Remember your manners."

"Didn't he?" persisted Green despite his wife's admonition.

"Not crackers, exactly," said Bella, "if by that you mean he went mad."

"Crackers," retorted Green, "means what you want it to mean. Acting daft—like going out late at night for no reason. Off his trolley—like wearing odd socks. Nuts—like talking rubbish. Any of these and more."

"Strange."

"OK. Strange. What did he do during that last week?"

"He developed insomnia."

Green put his tankard down. "You'd better explain, Bella. Fully, please, because though you may know what you're talking about, we don't. So no short-cuts. Put everything in."

Bella settled herself more comfortably in her chair. "Haydn

40

Prior was as level-headed a man as anybody could wish to meet. Believe me, I would not have consented to marry him had he not been."

"Now that I really can believe," said Green.

"I will vouch for what Mrs Bartholomew has just told you," said Pulker. "Prior was a steady man."

"Was," said Green. "Until when?"

"As I said, until about a week before his death. I first became aware of it because he began to look tired. I asked him why, and he told me he had not slept for two nights. Now, that in itself was extremely odd because Haydn always claimed to have slept extremely well and he had never had to resort to any form of sleeping pill. He took a whisky last thing at night, but he was by no means a heavy drinker of the sort that falls into a drunken stupor."

"Sudden insomnia?"

"Out of the blue, with no warning."

"He saw his doctor?"

"At my insistence. He didn't want to, but he looked washed out."

"What did his doctor do?"

"He gave him a prescription for sleeping pills. Haydn took the prescribed doses at the correct times."

"With what result?"

"Certainly not the desired one. He did not sleep."

"Did he go to see the doctor again?"

"No."

"Why not?"

"Because, like a lot of men, he was stubborn. I tried to persuade him, but he very rarely saw a doctor and regarded it as a weakness of character to need medical attention."

"George is just like that," said Wanda. "He was half dead last winter but wouldn't see a doctor or take a day off work."

"Quite right, too," said Green. "There aren't many of us left. But let's not get bogged down with George. He's my boss and has detailed me to conduct this part of the enquiry. Only because he's one of the family, of course, and so wants an independent investigator to take his mother-in-law apart. But as he's present

41

and looking on, I've got to make a good job of it, otherwise I shan't create a good impression. So no more interruptions, sweetie."

"Sorry," laughed Wanda. "I should have recognised the technique. I was subjected to it myself. But you were both so considerate in the way you went about it that it's hard to realise you are actually once again on parade."

"Thanks." Green turned to Bella. "You said Mr Prior wouldn't go to see his doctor again."

"I tried hard to persuade him, because he was falling apart in my presence. But he kept rambling on about the time-scale."

"Time-scale? Was he lucid?"

"Sometimes I thought not. But the time-scale he kept mentioning merely meant it was too soon to see the doctor again. He'd had two completely sleepless nights. So he saw the doctor. Both he and the doctor thought that was a bit soon, but forty-eight hours without sleep had taken its toll. I could see that. That is why I insisted on the visit to the doctor. He got the pills. They didn't work. Haydn said we had to give them time to work. Forty-eight hours was not giving them long enough to prove their worth, and consequently it was too soon to see the doctor again. That was his time-scale. But the last time I saw him he'd had no sleep for four nights. That's about a hundred hours or more, and for a man who was accustomed to sleeping regularly and well, that was a long time."

Green nodded. "I can see your point. He obviously needed his sleep, otherwise he wouldn't have slept well all his life. Presumably, with people who are accustomed to not sleeping well, four nights of deprivation aren't as bad as they turned out to be for Mr Prior." He looked round the assembled company. "Do you sleep well, Mr Pulker?"

"I must confess to taking Valium occasionally to help me sleep. But I am by no means a nonsomniac."

"Nonsomniac?"

"People who sleep very little or not at all."

"There are such people?"

"Yes," said Masters. "Napoleon, for example, slept very little and managed to keep going. By that I don't mean that he consciously only allowed himself to sleep for a few hours a night. That is what his body demanded and his mind supplied. But when it comes to total nonsomniacs, I am unable to help you. My guess is, however, that they do not exist among healthy people though I know there are reported cases of perfectly healthy people who sleep, on an average, for no more than forty minutes a night."

"Thanks for the information." Green returned to Bella. "As I see it, those who are accustomed to little sleep get along very well on their short ration. But those accustomed to long hours of snoring their heads off begin to suffer immediately they are deprived of their full eight hours. Now, Mrs B., you said, a few moments ago, that sometimes you thought Mr Prior was not lucid and that he was falling apart in your presence. That may be a good general description and gives us all some idea of how he must have seemed to you, but I'd like more exact details of what he did, what he said and how he looked. And, don't forget, you said he was burbling on about a time-scale. Can you link the details I asked for with his time-scale idea?"

Bella looked at him with approval. "It hadn't occurred to me to do so before, William. But it just shows how clever questioning will elicit answers—even information—that one didn't realise one knew."

"Are you talking to gain time?" asked Green. "Or to sidetrack me for some reason, or what?"

"In order to marshal my thoughts, dear man. You have asked me to list the mental and behavioural effects upon Haydn and to link them with the days as they passed. A tall order, but I can safely say there was a sort of progression. Yes, definitely a progression."

Green nodded. "That sounds logical."

"He looked tired, but he wasn't drowsy. I'm talking about the time when I was urging him to see the doctor after missing two nights' sleep. I can best describe his condition by saying that I expected—from looking at him—that there would be lapses of awareness."

"How do you mean?"

"That he would nod off in my presence."

43

"He was still perfectly lucid at this time?"

"Perfectly. But tired. He gave me the impression of what I imagine political prisoners must seem like in Russian gaols. Those who are allowed to fall asleep and then are immediately awakened. Before they become absolutely wretched of course."

"Fine. Then he went to the doctor. Got his pills. Took them. Didn't sleep. What happened?"

"I called on him. After that third night, his eyes had grown wider. I mean, he seemed to stare at me, and he seemed to be more aware of noise. I know he almost jumped out of his skin when I snapped my handbag shut." She paused for a moment. "I think that was all on that day. Certainly there were no signs of disorientation, though he was too disinterested to converse in his usual rational manner."

"He was irrational?"

"No. But he did not pursue a conversation to the logical conclusion as he would normally have done. He became monosyllabic and a bit muttery."

"Did you try to persuade him to see the doctor again on that day?"

"Not persuade. I suggested it. But he said the drugs must be given a chance to work and the doctor would think him a fool if he went back inside twenty-four hours."

"Good. Now, Bella, you must have asked him what he did during the night. Did he go to bed? Did he read? Make pots of tea?"

Green did not miss the effect this question had on Bella. She shied away from it ever so slightly, and then answered a bit too quickly: "He did all those things. Oh, and he took a warm bath because he thought it would relax him and make him drowsy."

Green smiled knowingly at her. "What are you hiding from me, love?"

"Hiding? Nothing."

"I'll take your word for it. I suppose you went to see him the next day, after four nights without sleep?"

"Yes. Yes, I did."

"You're not helping," accused Green. "You said you weren't

keeping anything back about the third night. I believed you. But something happened on the fourth night, didn't it?"

Bella nodded miserably.

"What?"

"He rang me up at twenty past two in the morning."

"Was he ill?"

"I immediately came to the conclusion that he was slightly delirious, even paranoid."

Green frowned. "What he said didn't make sense?"

"Not his usual clarity. But I did make sense of it, eventually."

"Please tell us all about it."

"I wasn't the first person he had phoned that night."

"In the early morning?"

"Yes. He had been trying to phone me, but heaven knows what numbers he had dialled. Quite naturally, I suppose, the people he had awakened were not too pleased. They didn't know him, and he asked for me. They either couldn't or wouldn't help him. I suppose their attitude gave him the idea that he was being persecuted. When—quite how, I don't know—he finally managed to reach me, he said that there was a devil after him."

"He was hallucinating?"

"I didn't think so. I didn't get the impression that he was seeing things, but rather that he was possessed in the biblical sense."

Pulker shook his head and muttered: "Poor fellow! Poor, poor fellow!"

Green ignored him and continued to question Bella.

"What did he want from you?"

"Comfort, I suppose."

Green nodded. "Very natural. You were able to calm him?"

Bella sat up rather straighter. "I told him I would go to him immediately. So I got out of bed, dressed, and drove to his house."

"Please go on."

"I made him go to bed, and I sat with him."

"For the rest of the night?"

"Until half past eight in the morning."

"Did he sleep?"

"Not a wink. But whilst I was there he was lucid and he had

neither hallucinations nor any sense of being persecuted. He lay there, eyes open, looking a thoroughly fatigued man. For the most part he appeared disinterested in me and yet my presence seemed to be a comfort to him. I got a little information from him as to how he felt from time to time. He told me at one time that he felt like the man in the iron mask."

"He what?" exclaimed Green. "What do you reckon he meant by that?"

"That he had a sensation of pressure round his head."

"Anything else?"

"He experienced a tingling sensation in his skin."

"As though there were creepy-crawlies all over him?"

"No. That would have been hallucinatory, wouldn't it? No. Tingling was what he said. I took that to mean a sort of stinging sensation, probably very slight. Not the tickling sensation of crawling spiders."

"I get you, love. Anything else?"

"Noises in his ears. I told you he had become very sensitive to noise. That was all, I think."

"Right. Now for the big question. Why didn't you call a doctor?"

"I ought to have insisted. I wanted to. I suggested it, but he forbade it."

"Why didn't you overrule him?"

"Because he promised to visit his GP in the morning. And as he seemed to be fairly settled with me sitting beside him, I thought it as well not to excite him by phoning the doctor."

"Right. Now I know he was your fiancé, but why did he ring you? What about the other people in his house?"

"He was alone."

"That seems strange to me. A wealthy man, living alone and looking after himself? His first wife had been dead for several years. Didn't he have a housekeeper?"

"He did have until shortly after our engagement. Mrs Hapgood had been with him for several years, but had wanted to leave for some time."

"Was there trouble between them?" asked Green suspiciously.

"Nothing like that. Mrs Hapgood wanted to join her married daughter in Australia, but she had hung on until Haydn should get himself another housekeeper. She was devoted to him and wouldn't leave until she was satisfied he was going to be well looked after. Of course, when Haydn and I decided to marry, the situation altered. Besides myself, there would be Ena Cully . . ."

"This Ena Cully, she knew she would be staying with you?"

"Of course. There would never be any question of my parting with Ena Cully."

Green glanced across at Masters before continuing his interrogation. "How long before he died did Mrs Hapgood go?"

"About a month before. She was anxious to be gone, and as Haydn had a cleaning woman who went in each morning to keep the house straight, make his bed and attend to his laundry, she was satisfied he would be well-looked after until he remarried."

"Where would you have lived?"

"That was our one area of disagreement. He wanted to keep his house, whereas I wanted to stay here. It would have been decided amicably, of course, eventually. We just let the question slide for the time being."

"And you had actually told Ena Cully she would be staying?"

"Oh yes, we had. She was the first person we told of our engagement, and Haydn himself told her he hoped she would stay with us."

"She was happy to do so?"

"She was very happy, but like me, she wanted to stay in this house."

"I see. Thank you." Green drained the last of his beer before proceeding. When he put his tankard down, Masters rose to refill it. As he passed Green, he said, so quietly as only to be heard by his assistant: "Keep it up, chum." Green nodded almost indiscernibly and turned again to Bella.

"What did the doctor say and do when Prior visited him the next morning?"

"Nothing. Haydn didn't go to him."

"You mean he wilfully broke the promise he had made to you during the night?"

"No. He rang the surgery. There is an appointments system. The receptionist asked him what the trouble was. Haydn, apparently, merely replied that he couldn't sleep. The girl didn't consider that very urgent and told him she couldn't fit him in at the morning surgery session, but he could go to the evening surgery at five twenty-five."

"Go on."

"Haydn didn't turn up."

"What did he do?"

"I don't know. The last I saw of him was when I left him that morning. I rang in the middle of the morning to hear what the doctor had said, and he told me what I've just told you. Perhaps I was at fault in not ringing the doctor myself and insisting that he visit Haydn, but the man was not my GP and though I was about to marry Haydn, I was neither a member of his family nor a close relative so I had no standing or authority to demand a call. Besides the appointment had been made, and Haydn, though he sounded weary, seemed to be in full possession of all his faculties. I invited him to lunch, but he declined, saying he had reserved his table at The Grange . . ."

"He'd reserved a table for lunch? In his state?"

"He went to The Grange every day for lunch. Or, rather, he had done since Mrs Hapgood left. I would have been very happy to have him here for lunch, but he preferred to go to The Grange at midday and to visit me for his evening meal. We were not always here, of course. We dined with friends or in Salisbury or Amesbury or at one of the inns round about. He was away from Cardinal quite often, of course. Just for the odd night or two each time."

"On business?"

"Yes."

"You told us he didn't keep the appointment with the doctor in the evening. Did he give any excuse for not doing so?"

"To me? No. I never saw him again. Because of his illness we had made no arrangement to meet that evening, but I had expected him to ring me after he had seen the doctor. When he hadn't either rung me or visited me by eight o'clock, I rang his house. There was no reply. I tried again half an hour later, but with no success, so I bundled Ena Cully into the car with me and we went to the house."

"Why, exactly?"

48

"Because I thought the doctor could have done something to relieve the insomnia. If Haydn had been doped, the first thing he would have done in his state, after he got home, would be to fall asleep and remain asleep, no matter what happened, for a good many hours. I thought his sleep was probably too deep to be disturbed by the telephone bell, so I went to see that all was well."

"What did you discover?"

"The house locked and in darkness. I still thought Haydn would be inside, sleeping, but the last thing I wanted to do was make a racket to waken him."

"So you left it at that?"

"I didn't like doing so. I had a nagging fear all was not well. So when I got home, I did what I should have done two, if not three, days before. I rang Haydn's doctor."

"What did he say?"

"He was very cagey about discussing Haydn with me. At last I managed to persuade him that I was not asking questions about one of his patients, but giving him vital information. So he listened to me. It was all news to him, and he was shocked. Finally, he confided in me to the point where he told me Haydn had not turned up for his appointment at evening surgery."

"You must have been worried sick," said Doris Green. "What did you do?"

"There was little I could do. I suggested to the doctor that he should inform the police that Haydn was missing, but he wouldn't go along with that. He declared that the police would not concern themselves with an adult male who had made himself scarce, let alone for only a matter of a few hours. Their attitude would be that he was free to disappear should he choose to do so, without the police hounding him down."

"Quite right," said Green.

"But Haydn was a sick man."

"That could have made a difference, but as his doctor hadn't seen him, he couldn't vouch for Prior's condition. Let's face it, Bella, a doctor would look a bit of a nana if he were to tell the local bobbies that the man was ill, not having seen him. Even on your say-so."

"You may have your rules and regulations, William, but I am uninhibited by such red tape. I rang the police myself and explained."

"Oh, yes?"

"They listened to me very courteously. Of course they all knew Haydn."

"I expect they said they would keep an eye open for him."

"Yes."

"But they made no promise to mount a special search?"

"They said they would enquire if anybody had seen him."

"What about his other friends? Didn't it occur to you that he might have fetched up at some other house?"

Bella's eyes opened in surprise. "The thought never struck me."

Green grinned. "Did you look to see if his car was at his own home?"

Again Bella was surprised. "No. It didn't occur to me to look in the garage. It certainly wasn't in front of the house where Haydn usually left it until he put it away for the night."

Green turned to Pulker. "Where was the car found?"

"In the garage at the house."

"So it could have been that he was out and about on foot at nine o'clock when Bella called, or he could have been away in the car at that time, after which he came back and garaged it and then went walk-about."

"Is that important?"

"I don't know what is important and what isn't—yet. But when he died he had no coat on. I'm inclined to think that he couldn't have been out for at least five hours at night without a coat. But I don't know. It was a windy autumn night. Was it cold, Bella?"

"My reply to that is that it was about average. Certainly not biting cold."

"It would help if we knew his movements that evening." Green turned again to Pulker. "What had the post-mortem to say? Had he eaten that night?"

"I'm afraid I can't help you there. I haven't seen the pathologist's report. There really was no reason why the police should inform me of such detail."

Green inclined his head. "We'd like to see it. George and I can't ask for it. Can you?"

"I can try to get a copy for you. It may not be easy, but I am on good terms with the Salisbury police. They may question why I should ask for it . . ."

"They will. Have no fear of that. Now, had you been Sid Lunn's solicitor, it would have been different. You would have seen the report as of right."

Masters grinned to himself. He could see Green's tactics. Pulker took the bait.

"Ah!"

"Yes?"

"Sibbald is acting for him."

"And?"

"I know Sibbald quite well. A most amenable young man. I could perhaps . . . but would it be ethical?"

"Quite ethical," Green assured him. "You're not involved in the case. Not acting for the prosecution. That's the Crown's job."

"Just so. And an excuse for seeing the report?"

"Well I don't know that I can give you one. You'll think of something. And if you don't mind, do it pretty sharpish, because George and I will be away by Monday."

Pulker frowned, as if to indicate that he disapproved of such unseemly haste. The law's delays . . . how could he possibly do it before Monday? As if he could read these thoughts, Green asked: "Where does this Sibbald character practise?"

"In Salisbury. Not more than a stone's throw from my own premises."

"Goody! Make it tomorrow morning."

"But . . ."

"No buts, chum. Where's your office? I haven't been in Salisbury for years, but I used to go to a cinema that looked as if it had been built out of an old building on the corner of the square. There was a café across the way where we could get a cuppa and a wad, near a bus stop."

"Then you will know approximately where my office is. Not above a hundred yards from there." Pulker gave instructions for reaching his office and then asked: "Why are you interested?"

"Because George and I will be in there at ten tomorrow morning to see the report."

Pulker looked vaguely unhappy. "I shall just have to lay my cards on the table. Explain that Mrs Bartholomew, as Haydn Prior's fiancée, has got it into her head that she would like to see the report, not because she bears Lunn any ill-will; rather the contrary. Confess I can never understand how the ladies' minds work and hope he will help me to pander to a client's whim."

"Just the job. Say you'll do the same for him sometime, and give him a bottle of Scotch for favours received."

Pulker looked pained at the thought that Green supposed the law's favours could be bought for so paltry a sum, but nevertheless nodded his head in agreement.

"That's that then," said Green, "unless anybody has anything he or she would like to ask."

Masters cleared his throat. Green said: "I thought as much. Now George is going to wade in."

"Not very deep. You've covered a great deal of ground, Bill, so why should I get wet?"

"Come on. Out with it?"

"I want to ask about Haydn Prior's appetite."

"His what?"

"When I get thoroughly tired, I go off my food."

"I hadn't noticed," said Wanda. "When was the last time you refused a meal?"

"You shouldn't have got married, George."

"He's right, though," said Doris Green. "You do get past food when you're tired."

Masters let the chat subside and then went on: "As I understood it, Prior was literally dropping with fatigue. Natural enough after four or five days and nights without a wink of sleep. Yet he went to The Grange each day for lunch and as often as not, came to this house for an evening meal. What was his appetite like, Bella?"

"It wasn't good during those last days, George. He tended to pick at his food, and yet I got the idea that he seemed to welcome meal times as something definite to do. Something fixed and normal. As though in a topsy-turvy world he could find something solid and rational to hang on to. Does that make sense?"

There was a murmur of understanding.

52

"Also, I believe he knew he had to eat to live. After Mrs Hapgood left, he never ate breakfast. She used to prepare it for him, but when he was left alone he never prepared anything more than a cup of coffee for himself. In fact, he ate nothing at home. So I suppose that the two meals he had each day were necessary. And they were never large meals. So, though his appetite definitely fell off, he still ate. He loved soup for instance and always took that, but he'd never touch a sweet."

Masters thanked her, and Green asked: "What was the point of that, George?"

"To me, the fact that he could eat two meals a day was so surprising that it stuck in my mind. That's all."

"Anything else?"

"Yes. How did he keep going? He was not a young man. He'd been awake for well over a hundred hours, yet he could jump up in the middle of a wood, frighten a poacher and then, after being wounded, run heaven knows how far to the road before his heart packed in. That isn't the action of a tired man. Not of a thoroughly tired man."

Green ran his hand over his chin. "You heard Bella."

"Yes. But most of what she said concerned his state of mind rather than his physical state. A fatigued mind in a not over-tired body. It's a paradox, but that's what it seemed like to me."

"I'll grant you that. His mental tiredness showed on his features. And that's complicated matters for no good reason that I can think of."

"It could explain why he thought he was possessed of a devil. A power that could play tricks with a tired mind and keep a body active and hungry despite no rest for days on end must seem like a fiend incarnate to the victim."

"You're beginning to make me shudder," said Doris Green.

"Mr Pulker will be afraid to drive home," said Wanda.

"I am beginning to think so," said the solicitor. "I never for one moment realised that our senior detectives—excellent though I have always considered them to be—would probe so deeply, indeed could probe so deeply into an affair with which they are totally unfamiliar and concerning which there is such a dearth of known fact. That they should, from such slender beginnings, de-duce what I have just heard, is indeed frightening. It makes one wonder what unpleasant facets of human, or inhuman, nature may lie just below the surface of seemingly normal, everyday life."

"That's the job," said Green. "Like every other, you get more adept at it. And the better you get, the more of its drawbacks you uncover. George particularly. He has a peculiar mind."

Almost immediately after this, Pulker took his leave, with Green reminding him that Masters and he would be at the solicitor's office at ten in the morning. The ladies, too, decided to go to bed. Masters held Green back for a final nightcap.

"Bella is right," said Masters, pouring the drinks. "Something stinks."

"If we've got the facts straight."

Masters joined Green at the fire. "You were wondering that all through your interrogation, weren't you?"

"Too true. That's why I wanted to pressure Pulker into getting the pathologist's report. It may tell us nothing new, but at least it will be one bit of material evidence and it should confirm something of what we've heard."

"This son that's turned up?"

"Too opportune for me."

"And me. We're faced with the old problem concerning him."

"Which one? Why didn't he make himself known to his father, you mean? Particularly after Mrs Prior's death?"

"That. Which is suspicious enough in itself. But we reckon we know the answer to that one, and that is that Prior could prove he wasn't the father. No, I meant that whereas Prior's death could be swallowed had the son not turned up, now he has we have to ask ourselves if it is not very strange that Prior should die before he could will his money to a new wife. Isn't that a little too opportune for Gooding?"

Green nodded.

"We'll have to show he knew Prior was going to marry Bella to get that one to stick, though. That is if you're assuming that Gooding was in some way connected with Prior's death."

"That was what I was postulating."

"He lives in France. Even you and Wanda didn't know. It wasn't announced in the papers, like Prior's death."

Masters finished his drink. "Does Gooding's appearance give us cause to approach the local police?"

"Not that alone. If we come up with one fact . . ."

They went to bed.

CHAPTER III

"THE TIMES I had here!" said Green, looking about him after they had parked the car and were making their way towards Pulker's office. Wanda and Doris Green had travelled into Salisbury with them and had gone off to look at the shops and view the cathedral. "You know, George, the war was bloody awful and nobody in his right mind would ever want to repeat it, but most of us who came through it have some good memories."

"Distance lending enchantment?"

"Not that. At least not entirely. I was conscious of enjoying life at the time. On the whole. There were bits I'd prefer to forget, of course."

"You were a born soldier, Greeny. You took to it. Others didn't."

"Maybe," answered Green. "I'm not going to argue, because there are popular views about such things these days that make me sick."

"I know. For myself, I think I would have preferred to serve, but only in wartime, when it was active service. I couldn't visualise myself as a peace-time soldier. But your attitude has always surprised me. For a die-hard old Lefty like you to believe in the armed forces is a bit unusual."

"Aye, I know. But there it is. And here's Pulker's office."

They climbed the narrow stairs which led to the upper floor of the old house. Nothing had been done in the way of alterations to turn the place from a former dwelling into an office, and in places it looked as though the Victorian wallpaper was still there.

"Modern!" grunted Green, leading the way. "I don't know how these solicitors get away with it under the Shops and Offices Act. It's as bad as some of the Civil Service buildings."

Pulker must have heard them coming. As they reached the

landing, he appeared in a doorway. "Good morning, gentlemen. This way please. I'm afraid I have no staff on duty on Saturday mornings, but I have got a surprise for you."

"Oh, yes! What?" asked Green.

"Mr Sibbald is here."

"Damn," said Masters. "We could be letting ourselves in for trouble by meeting him."

"Not to worry," murmured Green, and led the way into the office.

Pulker made the introductions.

"It must be clearly understood," Masters said to Sibbald, "that we met by chance."

Sibbald grinned. He was gingery fair, with close-curled hair and a freckled face. He was square-built and grinned easily. "Don't worry, Superintendent. I fixed it. I've known of you for a longish time, you see, and . . ."

"I know," said Masters. "I recognise your face. From some years back. Were you articled to a London solicitor who was acting for one of the villains I helped to send down? I seem to remember you were sitting next to somebody instructing counsel in court."

Sibbald seemed pleased at Masters' feat of memory. He went on: "When Geoffrey told me this morning that you were coming to his office, I was absolutely delighted. You see, I was calling to see him because I wanted to photocopy this document." He pointed to an envelope on Pulker's desk. "Geoffrey has a photocopier, but I haven't. I thought I could get my document and meet you, Mr Masters, at the same time. Unfortunately, we find Geoffrey's copier is playing up and there is no member of his staff here to put it right. But I would have loved a chat with you, Mr Masters. Not about anything in particular. Just a chinwag about how things are in town. But as the machine isn't working, and you gentlemen obviously have business to discuss . . ."

"Wait, wait!" said Pulker, coming in on cue. "I think I'm right in saying that one of our department stores here has a photocopier." He turned to Green. "They charge something like five pence a page. If Sibbald is agreeable, you and I could go and photocopy his document for him and he and Mr Masters could have their chat.

It seems a pity not to do Sibbald a small service . . ."

"Quite," said Green wrily. "We could probably get a cup of coffee, too, if there's a café in the store."

"What an excellent idea. What do you say, Sibbald?"

"I'd be delighted." He put his hand in his pocket and brought out a handful of coins. "Let me give you the money for the machine. There are three pages to copy . . ." He handed over three 5p pieces. Pulker accepted them very solemnly, then he and Green departed.

Sibbald grinned at Masters. "You and I have not discussed that document, Superintendent. Nor will we. You don't even know what it is."

Masters inclined his head. "But our chat is to be the quid pro quo for a small service rendered by you to Mr Pulker?"

"No. I have rendered him no service. Should he wish to avail himself of some opportunity I may have presented him with— inadvertently—then I shall be happy to have been of service."

Masters filled his pipe with Warlock Flake from a brassy tin. "Tell me, Mr Sibbald, when you accept service, I take it you are prepared to go to all legal lengths to help your client?"

"It is my duty to do so."

"Quite. We in the police are a little more constrained. We have a sort of code of conduct."

"I think I understand. You, particularly, members of Scotland Yard, have to be officially invited before you can intervene in any case outside the Metropolitan Police area."

"Exactly."

"Does that code forbid conversation about a case with which you are not directly concerned?"

"With an officer of the court—such as yourself—who may be involved in that particular case, yes. A fact already well known to you, as, I think, your little subterfuge has shown."

Sibbald grinned again. "I don't know what you are up to, or Pulker for that matter. But I know and trust Geoffrey. What I know about you leads me to believe that I should trust you, too. I am certain that Geoffrey would never do anything which was not in my best interests—and hence, those of my clients. So I did not question either motive or reason when he asked to see a certain

58

document in which—in the normal course of events—he would have no direct interest. I would have shown it to him without reservation."

"That is exceedingly courteous of you."

"He's a good old stick."

Masters laughed. "That is as good a reason as any."

"Why not? But when I heard that he had met you last night and was expecting to see you this morning, at the same time as he hoped to have my document in his hands . . . well, I'm pretty thick, but my olfactory organ is all right."

Masters laughed again. "As I said, you're a good-natured man, Mr Sibbald. But don't be too trusting."

"How do you mean?"

"I, for instance, should the need arise, would not necessarily work in the best interests of your client."

"Truth would be your objective?"

Masters nodded. "Without fear or favour."

"And if my client were to want nothing but the truth to come out?"

"I was careful to say not necessarily."

"I noted that. But I would like to ask you for a bit of general advice, Mr Masters."

"I know—or think I know—what you are going to ask me."

"I suppose you do. If a man in trouble is anxious for the truth to be discovered, but can find no means of persuading those in authority that there is something to be uncovered, what then?"

"When the police feel they have an open and shut case and can see no good reason to probe further?"

"What will persuade them?"

"Nothing, unless force of argument will achieve it."

"It seems a bit one-sided to me. The weight of the police force against a man—as opposed to neutral, I mean."

"It's a problem, Mr Sibbald. A good policeman should look below the surface. But some officers are not good policemen, even though they may be good men. They suffer from the faults that afflict us all—prejudice, indolence, prejudgement, blindness . . . the lot. Because they are human. And humans are not perfect."

"So I can do nothing?"

"You have done something, Mr Sibbald."

"I have? What?"

"Asked Mr Pulker to stat a document for you. Cast your reports upon the photocopiers and who knows what the results may be."

"I see. Ask no questions, but wait and see."

"You could be lucky. Could be."

"And that is all you can tell me?"

"I have told you nothing, and it would be folly to suppose I have or, indeed, to interpret my words in any way other than to accept them at their face value."

Again Sibbald grinned widely. "But I can put what construction I like on the fact that you are here. Oh, I know you have come down to visit Mrs Masters' mother. But calling to see a solicitor on a Saturday morning, and not even her solicitor, at that . . ." He shrugged to suggest that Masters' actions spoke volumes.

Masters replied: "Mr Sibbald, I think we should be quite clear why I am here. It is not on business of my own. Mrs Bartholomew has asked me to help her. I am doing just that and nothing more."

Sibbald nodded. "I don't suppose I can invite you and Mr Green for a drink before you go back?"

"This morning?"

"At any time over the weekend?"

"We may like to take you up on that. If you were to give me your card, perhaps I could let you know."

"You mean it? I thought you would want to steer clear of me."

"Why?"

"To avoid possible charges of complicity over some case I have on hand."

"I haven't interfered in any case of yours, Mr Sibbald, nor will I."

"But I asked your advice."

"In general terms only. And any citizen can approach any policeman at any time for advice."

At that point the door opened and Pulker ushered Green into the office. The older solicitor handed Sibbald the envelope. "Your original and the photocopy you asked us to get for you are in there."

"Thank you."

"It's been a pleasure to be of service to you."

"Nice coffee they had in that restaurant, too," said Green. "I had a Chelsea bun with mine."

Sibbald had gone. Masters had the second photocopy of the PM report in his hand.

"Signed B. A. Orr. What is he? Hospital pathologist or forensic man?"

"Hospital."

"I was hoping against hope that Sibbald would tell me he had arranged for the defence to have a second PM carried out. But he didn't. So I presume this is the only one."

"You mean you didn't ask him?" queried Green.

Masters shook his head. "We didn't mention cases."

"I see. Well, what have we got there?"

"You didn't read it?"

"Hardly! In a store full of Saturday shoppers?"

"I suppose not. Orr states categorically that Prior died of cardiac arrest resulting from overvigorous exercise and shock."

"Can he say that?"

"He seems sure of himself. Cardioclasis due to cardiokinetic influences. And that means rupture of the heart caused by its action being overexcited."

"And the shock bit?"

"Inevitable shock. He claims there were clinical manifestations of an inadequate volume of circulating blood. Classic signs, in fact, of cardiogenic shock."

"I reckon he found what he thought he ought to find. I thought cardiogenic shock was an immediate thing. Give somebody a bit of bad news and he flakes out, due—and I'm quoting what I read about it—to a progressive discrepancy between the capacity of the arterial tree and the volume of the blood to fill it."

"That's certainly the definition of shock syndrome—the emotional trauma of mental shock. If Orr is adamant that cardiac arrest—from whatever cause—was the thing that killed Prior, we can't argue nor, I suspect, would any other pathologist."

Green grunted. "So there's no mileage for us there. What does he say about the gunshot wounds?"

"Very little. Numerous lesions . . . mostly superficial . . . none more than a quarter of an inch deep . . . none did damage to any vital organs though the area of the left eye suffered quite severely and the front of the scalp."

Pulker said: "But the shot would have caused shock."

"That I think is what Orr suggests. And what he will imply in court."

"Anything else?" asked Green, "or, being a hospital pathologist, did he just satisfy himself as to the cause of death and not bother about the contents of the organs?"

Masters turned the page. "Stomach . . . benzodiazepam. Metabolites of same in liver. That's our old friend Valium. So Prior took what the doctor ordered and . . . good heavens, what's this?"

"What's what?"

"Parachlorophenylalanine." Masters pronounced it slowly to get it out correctly.

Green said, laconically: "Aye, aye! Sounds nasty."

"Doesn't it, though! But Orr hasn't made any comment about it. Just a note to say that an amount consistent with an estimated dose of six grams daily had been ingested, as though it were a perfectly normal medicament. Which it may be, of course, as far as I know, but Bella made no mention of the fact that Prior's doctor had given him anything but Valium."

"So what do we do?" said Green. "Ask the doctor if he did prescribe this para something or another?"

"We can't do that. That would be interfering directly."

Green helped himself to a Kensitas from a battered packet. "Do you reckon the GP has seen this report, or been asked what he was prescribing for Prior?"

"If I were conducting the case, I would have asked him. But it wasn't in Orr's place to question him."

"May I say something?" asked Pulker.

"Please do," replied Masters. "We weren't excluding you. Feel free to say anything you've a mind to."

"As his man of affairs, I have the keys to Prior's house."

62

Masters waited for the solicitor to finish.

"There is no reason why we should not go there and look in Prior's medicine cabinet."

Green lopped the ash off his cigarette. "There's good thinking, for you. When do we go?"

"Shall I meet you there at two o'clock? I know you have to pick up your good ladies and get them home for lunch. That would give me time to do a few odd things that need my attention."

"Fine," agreed Masters. "Two o'clock it is. Meanwhile, would you mind if I were to make a call to London?"

"Help yourself."

"What's on?" asked Green.

"I'd like Reed and Berger to research parachlorophenylalanine for me. I've never heard of it. If I had, I would have remembered a name like that. You, yourself, said it sounds nasty. I'd like to know just how nasty."

"You think it is a poison?" asked Pulker.

"It can't be," said Green. "He wasn't poisoned. He died of a heart attack, and the pathologist didn't query the finding of the drug in the body. He would have done if it had been toxic—like arsenic or any of those things."

Masters made his call. Detective Sergeants Reed and Berger were resting, too, so the call had to go to Reed's home.

"Make a careful note of it," said Masters, spelling the name of the substance out a second time. "Everything you can get on it. References in text books, published papers or anything else you can find. I know it's Saturday, but do your best. You have the number where I'm staying. Call me there at six this evening. And Reed . . ."

"Chief?"

"Be prepared to have to come down here with what you get. Berger, too."

"Have you stumbled across something, Chief, or have you been asked to help the locals?"

"Keep it under your hat, Reed. Both of you. It may be something or nothing, and I don't want to start any hares."

"Got you, Chief. You've guessed the locals have made a porridge of something and you want to be sure of your ground before you intervene."

"Something of the sort. Six o'clock, sharp."

"We'd best be on our way," said Green, "otherwise our women-folk will have bought half Salisbury. See you at two, Mr Pulker."

"I shall come," said Bella, "to show you the way. George, cut my beef a little thinner, please. I like it like tissue paper and red."

Masters nodded and continued to carve the sirloin on the bone. "A little fat with it, Doris? Or are you a lean fiend?"

"As it comes, George, please. What a pleasure it is to see a real joint again, don't you think so, Bill?"

"Jedder," replied her husband.

"What? What did you say?" asked Wanda.

"Jedder."

Wanda looked puzzled. Green laughed. "You're not old enough to know, love."

"I have heard the word before," confessed Doris, "but it means absolutely nothing to me."

"Sasser, pommer," said Bella, surprising even Green, who roared aloud at hearing his hostess say the words.

"May we join in?" asked Masters. "Or is this some sort of private game?"

"Don't be huffy, George," said Bella, "and give William another Yorkshire pudding. Those little individual ones are no earthly good to a man of his build."

"You changed the subject," accused Wanda.

"The prerogative of the hostess at her own table," retorted her mother. "But if you insist on knowing what the words mean, all I can tell you is that they were in vogue for a while round about nineteen thirty. In those days I was a bit of a tomboy and ran wild with the village lads and lasses of my own age. They used the words. They are all expressions of approbation or approval. A nice-tasting apple could be jedder, sasser or pommer, or all three. Any treat or good thing was thus described. As to the etymology of the words, I don't think they have any. Certainly none that I know of. I don't suppose I've heard them used for forty-five years. William's remark recalled them. Yes, please, Doris, I would like the horseradish sauce, and there's plenty of gravy in the kitchen, so don't stint yourself."

Masters, having finished the carving, sat down and shook out his napkin. "So you'll be guide this afternoon, Bella. What about you other ladies? We can all get in the car."

"I'd like to come," said Doris. She turned to Bella. "Is it a jedder house?"

"Jedder, sasser and pommer, I'd have said. But, as I believe I've already told you, I don't care for it as much as this. It is too square, too solid and too Victorian. And it is isolated. Here, I'm in the village street and I can indulge my nosiness to my heart's content."

"How long to get there?"

"Inside ten minutes."

"Shall we say we will be ready to leave at a quarter to two?"

Brooksbank, Prior's home, was built of grey stone. It was double-fronted and stood alone, forty or fifty yards back from the road. It had a drive which divided, one arm leading to the garage at the side of and behind the house, the other to serve the front door. The gardens were not large, but having been left unattended for a few weeks and subjected to the ravages of autumn, they looked unkempt and uncared for. As Masters, with Bella beside him, eased the car into the drive, he saw Pulker standing on the low step before the front door.

"I waited for you. I thought you and Mr Green would prefer to search for yourselves."

Masters accepted the key from the solicitor and opened the front door. There was a small porch and then a glass-panelled screen door. This, too, was locked. When they finally reached the square hall, Masters looked about him.

"The feature of the house," said Pulker, "is the lacunar ceilings. In the time of the previous owners, one of the rooms upstairs was a nursery bedroom for a small boy. Each indented panel of the ceiling is papered with different pictures likely to appeal to a young man of five or six. Highly coloured aeroplanes in one, ships in another, bears in a third and so on. He could lie in bed looking up at them. Mr and Mrs Prior were so enchanted by it they refused to have it redecorated."

The furniture was still in place. The dust was visible, but not too heavy. Pulker led the way upstairs to Prior's bedroom.

"Valium," said Green, picking up a bottle from the bedside table and emptying a couple of the familiar blue and yellow capsules on to his palm. "But nothing else."

The two policemen then searched the house. The medicine cabinet in the bathroom held a few household remedies, all of them recognisable and all comparatively innocuous. In a kitchen drawer they found a tin of plasters, a bottle of aspirin and a tin of liver salts. Nowhere else did they find any sign of medicines or drugs.

"What conclusion have you come to, George?" asked Bella, when the search was over.

"There are several possibilities. Prior could have been taking parachlorophenylalanine and have emptied the bottle just before he died. In that case he could have put the container in the dustbin and that, I take it, has now been emptied."

Pulker nodded.

"Then we must consider the possibility that the substance was administered to Prior unbeknown to him. For what purpose I cannot guess, until I know what properties the drug has. But as the pathologist was obviously not unduly disturbed by discovering its presence in the body, for the moment I cannot assume that it was fed to him with the intention of killing him."

Bella said sharply: "Nobody feeds another person drugs without nefarious intent."

"Agreed, generally speaking. But we don't know that Prior was fed this substance. He could have had it in his possession from some previous illness—or even some illness of his wife. People do stupid things with drugs."

"Haydn was not stupid."

"Not stupid, but remember his condition during those last few days. He was probably capable of any illogical action."

Bella nodded. "You're right."

"You really must leave these things to the experts, Bella," said Wanda.

Bella turned to her daughter. "The minutiae, perhaps. But if I

66

had left this case to the local experts, what is coming to light now would never have been discovered."

"You can't blame George and William for that. Look how far they have got in less than twenty-four hours, and they are not even involved in the case officially."

"Now, girls!" said Green. "It's time we went home. Bella promised me buttered crumpets for tea."

As they stood on the doorstep, saying goodbye to Pulker, Masters asked him: "I want to know something from you or Bella."

"What's that?"

"Who knew of Prior's intention to marry Bella?"

"We didn't announce it in any of the papers," said Bella. "It was our intention to keep it very quiet. Not even everybody in the district knew. I didn't even tell you and Wanda."

"No," said Masters. "However, you invited Bill, Doris, Wanda and myself ostensibly for a short stay this weekend, but in reality to attend your wedding. Now couldn't Haydn Prior have got in touch with somebody—some old academic acquaintance, say—and asked him to come and be his best man? He would need a supporter, wouldn't he?"

Bella shook her head. "We were going to ask William to go to church with him. William and Doris with Haydn, you and Wanda with me. Then we were all going to have a jolly weekend together. Haydn and I would have gone on holiday after you'd returned to London."

"Neat," said Pulker. "Very neat and tidy. But that doesn't give Mr Masters a satisfactory answer. Nor can I help beyond saying that the vicar knew and he and Prior were arranging for a licence so that banns would not be called."

"Almost a conspiracy of silence," grumbled Masters. Then he paused, stepped back, and looked up at the house.

"Greeny!"

"Yes. What's up? You're looking agitated."

"Communication, Greeny! Prior was a ham radio enthusiast. There's his aerial up there. You examined his radio room."

"Yes. The one with the pictures on the ceiling. There were no drugs there."

Masters looked at Pulker. "Do you mind opening up again?"

"Not in the least. But may we know what for?"

"His radio log. There was one, wasn't there, Bill?"

Green nodded. "A hard-backed book. I just glanced inside. Full of call signs and brief messages."

"Let's look at it."

Pulker had returned to have tea with them. Green was saying to Wanda: "He's jammy, your old man. I've always said so. Let's look at the log, he says, and within two minutes he finds the entries he wanted. Prior was as tight-lipped as an inedible clam in normal life, but over the air he chatted like a sozzled flapper." Green grimaced and mimicked: "I'm very well. Very happy. I've got engaged to be married. How are you?" He snorted. "Loads of it. All about Mrs Hapgood leaving for overseas and all his domestic arrangements. Anybody anywhere in the five continents could have learned everything he wanted to know about Prior and his plans."

Pulker who had overheard this, asked: "But why should it matter? Why should the Superintendent want to know who knew about the proposed marriage?"

"Ask him," replied Green. "He's got some bee in his bonnet. And, knowing him, it's likely to be either the queen bee or the one carrying the most honey."

But Masters refused to be drawn, other than to say he had some idea chasing its tail inside his head.

"That's it, then," said Green. "We have to wait and see, like the pudding at home."

Bella asked: "What on earth does that mean?"

Green grinned. "When I was a kid and used to go home for dinner—no school lunches in those days—if I asked my Mum 'what's for pud?' she always answered 'wait and see', instead of plums and custard or whatever. So it became an in-joke between my dad and me. Wait and see pud."

"What comes next in your investigation?" asked Pulker, helping himself to another crumpet running in butter. "It really is a pleasure to me to get some insight into how you work."

"It's not usually like this," protested Green. "We don't normally

68

have a squad of onlookers and we always have the authority to investigate. This is like trying to run while carrying two buckets of sand."

"Thank you very much," said Wanda in mock indignation. She turned to Mrs Green. "Does Bill often describe you as a bucket of sand? Or me, for that matter?"

Pulker said hastily: "Oh, I feel sure Mr Green didn't mean . . ."

"Don't fall for it," Green counselled him. "She's pulling your old whatsisname. She knows very well what I mean, and so does my missus. All I'm trying to point out to you is that sooner or later—if we find cause for interfering in this case—we shall have to go official, and then there'll be trouble. Not only when we come to suggest it, but because the locals will know we've been sticking our noses in behind their backs before we approached them. Both will make them grumpy. And George is as much concerned by that aspect of the business as by the investigation itself."

"I see." Pulker turned to Masters. "How do you propose to . . . I suppose you would say ease yourself into the case?"

"There is only one way that I can think of, and that is to find some aspect of the package which concerns the Yard. Then we can start asking the local police enough questions to alert them to the fact that the case may not be quite so simple as they appear to suppose."

Pulker was about to reply when the phone rang. As it did so, the chiming clock on the mantelpiece struck six o'clock.

"Reed," said Green. "The lad's on time."

"May I answer it?" Masters asked Bella. She nodded her permission and he moved into the hall to take the call. Green followed him.

"Chief?"

"Speaking."

"Parachlorophenylalanine."

"What about it?"

"Quite a lot, Chief. But as it's such a mouthful to say, and it's known in the trade as PCPA, could we stick to that to make things easier?"

"Right. When you say the trade, to whom are you referring?"

"The forensic people. Doctors, technicians, researchers . . . the lot."

"What do they have to say about it?"

"Well, Chief, they were a bit choked because it was Saturday afternoon and we're not supposed to bowl fast ones on half days. But they told me a bit. I'll have to read it, because quite honestly I don't understand it and I don't know half the words."

"Go ahead. Take your time."

"First off, Chief, PCPA has been given to man, but no doctor would give much of it, because everybody who has ever used it knows it has a great many actions in the body, but nobody knows quite what."

"Is it a poison?"

"No, Chief. They told me it was an inhibitor of the biosynthesis of serotonin, whatever that means."

"Did you look up serotonin?"

"Yes, Chief. But I'm none the wiser. I'm quoting again. Serotonin. 5-Hydroxytryptamine, an amino acid derivative found in many tissues, which has diverse physiologic and pharmacologic activity. And before you ask what amino acids are, I'll tell you. They're a large group of organic compounds which are essential to life, because they are the end products of protein hydrolysis and from them the body resynthesises its proteins."

"Thank you. Hang on a moment. I'm taking notes." There was a short pause while Masters scribbled on the phone pad. Then—

"Are there drugs containing PCPA? Sorry. That's a stupid question. If it's been used in man, there must be."

"Yes, Chief. None that I can find in this country, but the States has one which has been given to patients with carcinoid syndrome . . ."

"Cancer?"

"Apparently not, Chief. Evidently, it's a tumour that's usually benign and commonly occurs in the appendix and the ileum—that's the lower portion of the small intestine."

"Fine. Go on."

". . . carcinoid syndrome, and some relief of symptoms, especially of diarrhoea—which I suppose the syndrome causes—has been reported. Hypothermia has also been reported and higher doses produce psychic side effects."

"Ah! Hold it! What sort of psychic side effects?"

"Sorry, Chief. Just psychic."

"Is the dose mentioned?"

"Doses of from two to four grams daily have been used. Higher doses—I suppose that means from about three and a half grams upwards—produce the psychic business."

"I've got that. Now, besides the States, who else uses the stuff?"

"I can't trace any drug other than the one I've been talking about, but there are some papers here and one of them talks about trials with it in France."

"France?"

"Yes, Chief, France. Has that sparked something?"

"Maybe. Is that all?"

"Unless you want me to read all these papers out to you, Chief."

"No. I want you to bring them down to me."

"Right, Chief. Now?"

"Just one thing to do before you come. Get on to Communications or anybody else who can help you to trace a ham radio operator, call sign FPX923X. I want his name and address."

"That's the Post Office, Chief."

"I know they issue the licences, but somewhere in our wigwam we have duplicate lists. One of the security offices will have them. Communications branch should be able to tell you which if they haven't got them themselves."

"Right, Chief. Berger's with me. Shall I bring him?"

"Hang on."

Masters turned to Green. "Would you like Berger to come?"

"To stay?"

"They may be of use."

"In that case, yes."

"Just nip in and ask Bella if she can put the two of them up for the night. There's a spare bedroom with twin beds in it, I think."

Green was back very quickly. "Bella says yes."

Masters spoke to Reed. "Both of you. Be prepared to stay till Monday, and come in your private car."

"Unofficial is it, Chief?"

"We'll wait up for you. You have the address."

After Masters had put the phone down, Green lit a cigarette.

"Coincidence?"

"May be sheer coincidence. A claimant to Prior's estate coming from France and the drug in his guts the subject of trials in France. It's mighty tenuous."

"But we can't ignore it."

"We can't ignore anything. But we've learned that PCPA isn't toxic. It just drives people crackers. And Prior was driven crackers. He knew it, too. When he told Bella he was possessed."

"Are we going to tell the crowd?"

"I'd rather not. If some of it has to come out, so be it. But I don't like having to parade all my thoughts. Having said that, there are some questions to be answered."

Green nodded, and the two of them rejoined the others.

"Well?" demanded Bella. "As you are bringing your sergeants here, I presume you have news for us."

"Not so's you'd notice, love," said Green, sitting beside his wife and stretching his legs. "A lot of mumbo-jumbo that even George can't understand. That's why he's having the sergeants come down with all the papers and a medical dictionary so's we can try to make a bit of sense of them."

Pulker got to his feet. "Ah, well, one can't live in a state of constant action. I regret to say I shall have to tear myself away from your lovely fire, Mrs Bartholomew . . ."

"Not yet, a moment, please," said Masters. "I mean, are you engaged for the evening?"

"No, sir. I am a bachelor and I was about to return to an empty flat. But I can't transgress on Mrs Bartholomew's hospitality on that account."

"You won't be transgressing. I believe we're going out to dinner. Didn't I hear you say you'd reserved a table somewhere, Bella?"

"A table for five at The Bandbox. It sounds ghastly, but it does a good steak. I'm sure we could change that to six."

"Fine, because I need the help of both of you."

"Oh! Excellent," said Pulker. "Both the invitation to join you and the prospect of work. What can we do?"

"It's the question of Prior's sterility."

"Oh! Now that's an area of his affairs I know little about."

"Maybe. But you were his solicitor and now you have a claimant to his estate who also claims to be his son whereas you have been reliably informed he could not father a child. You are in duty bound to sort these matters out."

"Agreed."

"Bella. Did Prior tell you when and where the tests on him were done? And by whom?"

"About thirty years ago, he said. He was married immediately he was demobilised after the war. They tried to have children for two or three years before deciding to submit to the tests."

"That would make it in forty-eight or thereabouts," said Green. "Exactly thirty years ago."

"Just so. He was tutor at Cambridge at the time, and I am certain he told me one of his colleagues carried out the tests."

"In a university laboratory?"

"I think he said a hospital. A teaching hospital."

"Addenbrooke's," said Green. "Almost certainly."

Masters nodded. "So his colleague would be a doctor of medicine. We'd get nothing out of hospital records at this hour on a Saturday night." He turned to his mother-in-law. "Did he ever tell you who were his closest, long-time friends in the academic field? Somebody he might have had to visit him here or with whom he corresponded?"

Bella shook her head. "Nobody in particular. There were so many—lots of them known names in their own fields."

"Pity."

"Perhaps I can help," said Pulker.

"Please," replied Masters.

"I am one of the executors of Mr Prior's will. The other is Doctor Durrant . . ."

"Doctor?"

"Not medicine. A Senior Doctor of Physics. One of those gentlemen who are so brilliant they stand out above even their own erudite colleagues and so are designated Senior."

"I see. They were long-term friends?"

"Certainly. But whether they were colleagues at Cambridge is another matter."

"Presumably you have been in touch with Doctor Durrant concerning Prior's estate?"

"Oh, yes. As an executor he has to be consulted over everything, and he will be particularly helpful over Prior's scientific bequests."

"He lives in Cambridge?"

"London."

"Can you call him?"

"Now?"

"Why not? It is only half past six. If he's going out for the evening, he is unlikely to have left home by this time."

"Very well. I know where he lives. With luck the exchange will find me his number."

"If not, I will ring the Yard. They'll get it."

"What am I to say?"

"Your excuse for ringing him is that you have just heard from this man Gooding, that he is claiming the estate, that he is arriving here on Monday and so you are having to make calls at unearthly hours.

"After that tell him you had been informed that Prior could not father children, that tests were done at Cambridge, and could he, Durrant, tell you who might have carried out those tests, so that you can try to check your facts before meeting Gooding on Monday. Brother executors and all that!"

Pulker nodded. "That sounds a very reasonable story."

"Because it's true."

"I'm unlikely to stray from the truth in professional matters of this kind, although . . ." Pulker grinned, ". . . although I must admit to the odd white lie at other times, when necessary."

"I'm sure. Can I leave it to you?"

"Now?"

"If you please."

Pulker went alone into the hall to telephone.

Bella Bartholomew said: "George, I have heard from Wanda on numerous occasions how good at your jobs you and William are. That you are relentless but considerate . . ."

Masters held up a hand in protest.

"Don't try to stop me. I discounted much of what my daughter told me, because I suspected she was a little starry-eyed where you two are concerned. Now, however, I realise she did not exaggerate. You two are relentless and imaginative. Would you also show how considerate you can be by pouring me a large schooner of La Ina and by performing a like service for everybody else present?"

"Before you change for dinner?" asked Wanda.

"Before. I'm not changing till I've heard what Pulker has to say. Thereafter, I promise you I will climb into some sort of glad rags inside five minutes."

"Just as well," said Green. "We shall want to be back for the sergeants."

"No, no, William. Don't let your enthusiasm run away with you. Ena Cully will admit them if we are not here. She will also feed them. Wanda will ask her to do that." She turned to Doris. "It's as well to let these men know that women can think and plan and arrange things, too. Ah! Thank you, George. I fear it must be a sign of degeneracy to be drinking sherry while the tea things are not yet cleared away, but I must say I feel ready for this."

As she drank, Green got to his feet and started to collect the cups and saucers. As his wife and Wanda made a move to help him he waved them away. "This is mine," he said. "Ever since I got here I've been wanting to meet this Ena Cully woman. Personally, I don't think she exists, but if she does, I'll tell her to expect the sergeants."

As Green went out with the tea trolley, Pulker came in. "See you soon, Geoff," said Green. "And it's your turn to dry up, so don't start gassing before I get back."

"If you say so," agreed Pulker.

Pulker was as good as his word and didn't start his report until Green returned, sat down, and picked up his drink.

"Dr Durrant was perturbed," he announced. "Very perturbed."

"About his pet charities losing Prior's dibs, you mean?"

"No, William. He doesn't fancy figuring in what may become a *cause célèbre*."

"He reckons that is what it will turn out to be?"

"That is what he fears, because he was well aware that his great friend Haydn Prior could not—as he put it—sire children. But he fears it may be an unprovable fact in a court of law."

"But the tests . . ."

"Were done thirty years ago. The techniques may not have been quite so sophisticated in those days as they are at the present time. He thinks that if Gooding were to get a modern research man to question those old tests—in the light of modern knowledge —a court could well rule that Prior was not necessarily totally sterile."

"Meaning that on occasion—with the right woman—he might have rung the bell?" asked Green.

"Just so."

Masters got to his feet to tap out his pipe at the fireplace. "Did you ask Durrant if he knew who did the tests?"

"Hayward, a young genito-urinary specialist. And Mrs Prior was investigated by the gynaecologist of the day, whose name Durrant does not remember."

"But he remembers Hayward?"

"All three of them were in the same set in those days. Hayward is still practising. He's at The London Hospital."

Green looked across at Masters. "Pull rank on them to give you his private address. You never know your luck. You might just get hold of him."

Masters nodded. "I'll try." He turned to Bella. "I hate using your phone as much as this, but then I hate trying to conduct an investigation by telephone. William will tell you that we get so much more to work on in face-to-face interviews."

Wanda got up and linked her arm in his. "Never mind, darling. I'll come and hold your hand."

The hospital preferred not to give Hayward's private number even to somebody who claimed to be a Detective Superintendent from Scotland Yard. Masters did not haggle. He called the Yard itself to get the information. It took the information room less than five minutes to look up Hayward's name in the Medical Register, get his initials correct and then to consult the telephone directory. With this information, Masters again rang London.

The phone rang and the receiver replied that the person answering was Mary Hayward.

"Good evening, Mrs Hayward. My name is Masters. Detective Superintendent Masters of Scotland Yard. I know this is a very inconvenient moment to call, but would it be possible to speak to Mr Hayward, please?"

"Can you tell me what it is about? My husband is a busy man, you know."

"It is a police matter, ma'am. It shouldn't take long."

"I'll see whether he will talk to you."

Masters covered the phone with his hand. "A right old protective battleaxe there. Why must women be so jealous of the phone calls their husbands receive?"

"He's probably late in getting ready to take her out."

The phone made a small sound as it was picked up. "Hayward, here."

"Good evening, sir. Mrs Hayward has probably told you my name is Masters."

"From the Yard, yes. What's it all about?"

"A friend of yours, the late Haydn Prior."

"Oh! Something wrong about that is there? His death was tragic. Of course, the police would naturally be looking into it. But I don't see how I can help. I hadn't seen Prior for six months or more."

"The circumstances of Mr Prior's death are not my immediate concern, Mr Hayward."

"No? What then?"

"Mr Prior died childless, apparently."

"No apparently about it. Poor old Haydn couldn't have fathered anything."

"So we are led to believe, sir. And yet a claimant has come forward."

"A claimant?"

"To his estate. A young man of twenty-nine who claims he is Prior's natural son."

"The answer to that, Superintendent, is extremely short."

77

"Quite, sir. But Dr Durrant, who is one of Mr Prior's executors, has raised a question."

"Christopher Durrant has? That's the trouble with these senior physicists. They're always asking questions. What's his problem?"

"Simply that you carried out sterility tests on Mr Prior . . ."

"I did. At Addenbrooke's in Cambridge. Must be thirty years ago now."

"Quite, sir. Dr Durrant wondered whether modern techniques might not invalidate tests done so long ago."

"I get his point, but the answer is no. I can say, without bumming my chat too much, Superintendent, that I'm one of the world's leading lights in that particular field. And I was then. Haydn Prior was completely incapable of spermogenesis. Don't get me wrong. He was apparently quite normal. He produced semen. But his trouble was a form of spermatacrasia which is a deficiency—in his case a complete deficiency—of spermatazoa in the semen. Even thirty years ago we were sufficiently advanced to determine that, Mr Masters."

"So Dr Durrant's fears are unfounded, and Mr Prior's solicitor can rest assured that the claimant, Gooding, is an impostor?"

"Certainly."

"Thank you. You have been most helpful. I apologise for ringing you at this time on a Saturday, but this young man lives in Paris and he has announced his intention of appearing to stake his claim on Monday morning, so I had to work quickly."

"Yes, yes. That's all right. But there's something . . ."

"Yes?"

"Gooding, you say?"

"Harry Gooding. Does it ring a bell, Mr Hayward?"

"Yes it does."

"In connection with Prior?"

"With me, actually. I'm trying to place it. Now, let me see . . ."

"Gooding would be his mother's name . . ."

"That's it! I've got it. Elsie Gooding. A nubile blonde. She was one of my nurses at that time . . ."

"The time you carried out the tests on Prior?"

"Yes. She was there at the time. Not long afterwards she suddenly left us. She was regarded in those days as an easy make,

78

if you get my meaning, Superintendent, and her hurried departure, I can remember, caused—we were young then—much speculation as to the identity of the father."

"You knew she was pregnant when she left?"

"Knew? Probably not for certain, but we were medical men."

"I see. But you can guarantee Haydn Prior was not the father of her child?"

"Categorically. On two counts. Physical incapability and the fact that Haydn Prior was so besotted by his own wife he'd never have looked at Elsie Gooding. Times were a bit different then, you know."

"Thank you, Mr Hayward."

"Not at all. Get in touch with me again if I can help. And I'll ring old Durrant for you and put his mind at rest—if you'd like me to."

"That would be very helpful. Thank you and goodnight."

CHAPTER IV

THERE HAD BEEN no time to discuss the conversation with Hayward before getting ready to go out to dinner. As Masters and Wanda had entered the sitting room, Green had looked up and enquired: "Corn in Egypt?"

To this Masters had replied that there were a few sheaves, he thought, but he would like to discuss them over dinner if everybody approved. Green agreed readily. He was enjoying himself to the full during this weekend, despite the role thrust upon himself and Masters by Bella. Doris, in her quiet way, seemed to be happy as long as her husband was happy. Wanda, however, was just a little put out that her mother should have encumbered George with what she privately thought of as a fight which he had been obliged to enter with both hands tied behind his back.

They had all gone upstairs to wash and change. Masters had hung back to show Pulker the bathroom. When he entered his bedroom, Wanda was standing in bra and pants, examining a pair of tights for flaws. The sight of her stirred Masters to an amazing degree, considering he saw his wife in just this or a similar state a dozen times a week. But she had only put one bedside lamp on. The light caught her very fair, longish hair. Pure gold shone. Her lithe figure: slightly tall, beautifully made and attractively, if slightly, tanned—just enough to prevent any of her skin which showed from having the too-pale, anaemic look which Masters loathed. He liked women's legs, but when hot weather arrived and they shed stockings and tights, but did not go to the trouble of making-up their legs, he was always reminded of undercooked suet pudding. Wanda's legs were tanned, and in the subdued light the little hairs shone gold. He closed the door and stood quite still to watch her. After a moment, as though missing his expected movement, she looked round at him. For a moment they stared at each other, and then she was in his arms.

As he held her, she said: "I don't want to go out to dinner."

"Nor do I, sweetheart. But don't tempt me. I'm finding it difficult enough to resist you as it is."

"Me, too."

"There's one comfort. In an hour or two I can put you to bed without keeping everybody waiting for dinner."

"I know. It's a nice thought isn't it?"

"A prospect, my beautiful. Now get yourself dressed or I shall forget all about Bella's wretched case."

"I'm sorry. It's a rotten trick to pull on you."

"Not if what she says is true." He released her and took off his jacket.

"And is it true?" she asked, drawing on the sheer nylon tights.

"Shall we say that for an apparently straightforward case, it has some remarkable convolutions."

She put on her slip and moved to the dressing table. "So you are not quite as cross about it as you might have been, had she just been starting a hare."

"Not cross. I just feel we could have done without it on our weekend off."

Despite its name, The Bandbox was discreet. Basically it had been an old inn. Now it had sprouted wings in stockbroker Tudor, but the architect had tried his best. None of the dining rooms was big —there were four or five of them—and each provided secluded tables. The old villagers who had been accustomed to using the place were no longer catered for. The prices ensured that. So did the decor. The spit and sawdust had given way to carpets and low wattage table lamps, chairs covered in red and tables boasting— to Masters' surprise—white tablecloths and linen napkins.

Bella's table—now changed to seat six—occupied the end of one room and, Masters noted, was sufficiently far from its neighbours to allow conversation with little fear of being overheard.

As they dealt with wedges of excellent pâté, Masters recounted his conversation with Hayward. Pulker was delighted. Waving a finger of toast about in the air to emphasise his words, he drafted out his plan of campaign for the meeting with Gooding on Monday.

"What happened about the birth certificate?" asked Doris Green. "You all seem to know, but I don't."

Her husband said: "Look, love, all births have to be registered. Usually the proud father does it. But that's something a girlie who's having an illegitimate baby is apt to forget. So it comes as a shock when she pootles along to the registrar and he asks her for details of the father. My guess is that this Nurse Gooding was caught on the hop and produced the first name she could think of."

"Why? Why not the real father's name?"

"Because, if what Hayward said is true, she slept around a bit and she might not have known which man was the child's father."

"But to give another man's name—one she knew could not possibly be the father, even if . . . if something had happened between them, is criminal."

"You're being delicate, love," said Green fondly.

"Maybe. But what I said is true."

"Of course it is," said Masters. "You're quite right, Doris. It has led, if not to blackmail, at least to a false claim to a very large sum of money."

"So why do it?" asked Green. "Was she scared that if she named one of the possibles and he got to know he'd cause trouble? Not a bit of it. She thought it would sound good to have a Cambridge lecturer as the father. Don't forget in those days members of university staffs were not the long-haired layabouts half of them are today. They were looked on as men of standing."

"While agreeing with all you say," said Wanda, "there is another possible explanation for her action."

"Let's hear it, love."

"If Nurse Gooding had been involved in the tests made on Mr Prior, she might have come to realise how sad the results would make him. He maybe spoke of it, or she guessed it. I don't know. But couldn't it have been a happy thought of hers—a kind one, if you like—to say that a fatherless child was his? In name only. Even if he never knew about it." She looked round the table. "Surely somebody understands what I'm trying to say."

"I do, love," said Green. "I'll take your explanation as the right one."

"And you, George?"

"I'll accept it, too, though I was thinking that it was probably wishful thinking on her part. What if she started to care very much for Prior—fell in love with him, if you like—while the tests were going on? Might she not have wished—desperately—that Prior had been the father? And having wished it, named him as some sort of wish fulfilment?"

"I like that, too," said Doris. She turned to Bella. "I'm a silly old romantic, but it is difficult to think of a girl with a new baby doing criminal things."

"We'll give her the benefit of the doubt," said Bella. Pulker agreed with her, adding that it was Miss Gooding's legal right to be so adjudged in the absence of evidence to the contrary.

Masters allowed the waiter time to get well away from the table before he said: "Now we ought to know if she is still alive, and if so, where she is. It could be that she married and now has a different name. I think, Bill, we ought to ask the Yard to look into it. The registry office . . ."

"Somerset House?" asked Bella.

"Not now, I'm sorry to say. They keep all records of births, deaths and marriages registered in England and Wales since early last century at the Office of Population Censuses and Surveys. It's in Kingsway."

"It doesn't sound half as nice and safe as Somerset House."

"Call it St Catherine's House," said Green, "and you'll not feel so bad about it." He turned to answer Masters. "It'll have to be Monday morning. But we can lay it on tomorrow so they'll get an early start."

Masters nodded. "If we could locate her before Mr Pulker's visitor arrives, so much the better."

"Why?" asked Wanda. "What can you say to her? You surely are not going to drag up something from the poor woman's past which she probably thinks is over and forgotten?"

"Making omelets without breaking eggs is impossible," said Green. "You can't have it both ways, you know, love."

"Have what both ways?"

Green carefully picked a lemon pip off his grilled sole, put it on the side of his plate and then licked his fingers.

"Come on, Bill," said Doris.

Green looked at Wanda. "If you were the mother of that fellow, Gooding, would you want him to fall foul of the police . . ." Green paused ". . . because of something you had done?"

"I had done?"

"By leading him to believe that Prior was his father."

"How do you know she did?"

"She put it on his birth certificate—a legal document."

"Oh."

"Yes! Oh! Nurse Gooding may have had an illegitimate baby. She may have put the wrong name on the certificate, but that doesn't mean she's any more dishonest than the rest of us. Don't you think she'd fight shy of being party to nicking umpteen score of thousands of pounds. If her son is bent—and we can't yet say he is because we mustn't prejudge him, even though we proceed as though we think he is a villain—it's a big crime he's trying on. I haven't a clue how much Prior was worth, but that house of his without the contents must be worth sixty thousand. Geoff, here, will tell you if there's more, which there must be, because inventors are like pop record artists, they get a rake off of a copper or two on every item sold."

"Quite right," said Pulker. "Prior's patents will be a steady source of income to his legatees for years to come."

"So," continued Green, "what will Nurse Gooding want? For us to steer clear and let her son end up in chokey, or for us to talk to her and save him? And, remember, it was you who said she was either kind to Prior or sweet on him. If we grant you that, as we did, why should she want to be party to pinching his worldly goods? It wouldn't be in character. So, lovey, somebody's got to make their minds up about this woman. If she's a villain we want to see her. If she's honest, she'll want to see us—after she knows why we called."

"I should keep out of this," said Wanda. "I know from experience how you and George can make bricks without straw."

"Be fair, poppet," said her husband. "Bill was being extremely logical."

"That's just what I mean," wailed Wanda. "You two are always so logical it makes the rest of us look like ninnies."

Green rose to the occasion. "If all ninnies look like you, dear, I'll settle for being a ninny any time. And so would half the rest of mankind."

"That's true you know, Wanda," said Doris seriously. "You are a very lovely girl. Such a heavenly figure."

"Thank you."

Bella interrupted. "So it is obvious we shall need to trace the Gooding woman and confront her with the facts. I take it that you expect her to confess to wrongfully crediting Haydn as the father of her child—in view of what we know. But what if she persists in maintaining the fiction?"

"Would blood-grouping help?" asked Pulker. "We know what group Prior was."

"Unlikely," replied Masters. "Unless Prior was of some rare group."

Pulker, looking a little sad that he could not announce that Prior was something other than group O, returned his attention to his plate. Masters replied to Bella. "If she is stubborn, then it will come to a legal battle between Nurse Gooding and her erstwhile chief, Hayward. And in that case, she will have to explain how, being a member of a team which had just pronounced Prior infertile, she managed to produce his son. If she had become pregnant by Prior, despite Hayward's findings, why did she not reveal the apparent miracle to Hayward? I think it fair to suggest that most nurses in her particular speciality would have done so."

"If only to show her boss he was wrong?" asked Green.

"I imagine she would be more condemnatory than that. Tearfully telling Hayward that he had said Prior couldn't when he could, as she had learned to her cost."

Green nodded and turned to the approaching waiter. "Have you got a sweet-trolley, lad?"

"Yes sir."

"Got anything interesting on it?"

"Such as, sir?"

"I fancy a bit of bramble and apple pie."

The waiter paused a moment. "Brambles, sir? They would be blackberries, would they?"

"Bang on, lad."

"In that case, sir, we might manage it. What I mean is, we have apple pie and we have stewed blackberries. If you were to have both . . ."

"Good idea. But strain the brambles well. I don't want any of the jizzer-rizzer."

The waiter inclined his head and went about his business. Bella said to Green: "You remind me of Queen Victoria, William. She knew what she liked and went for it."

"A great queen," said Green. "Now, where have we got to, George?"

"I think we are as far as we can go at the moment. We'll see what news the sergeants bring."

Pulker had not returned with them. He had said goodnight, immediately after dinner, with a firm promise from Masters that he would be kept informed of all that went on.

They reached Winterbourne Cardinal just before half past ten. Apart from some muted noise from The Grange, which still had all its lights blazing and, apparently, a goodly crowd of customers, the village was quiet.

The sergeants arrived ten minutes later.

"Sorry to be so late, Chief," said Reed as Masters opened the door to him. "But you know what it's like trying to get information on a Saturday night."

"Not to worry. Bring your bags in and then park the car at the side of the house." He pointed to the double gates beyond the dining room. "Just leave it in the open. There's no room in the garage."

"Right, Chief."

"Then, come in. We've got something for you to eat."

The sergeants joined them a few minutes later in the sitting room. Bella was the only one with whom they were not on fairly close terms, and even she was not a perfect stranger because they, too, had attended Masters' wedding.

It was Wanda who brought in the trolley with a covered dish

full of hot sausage rolls and another full of sandwiches. "I thought you'd rather have beer than coffee, but I can bring you a pot if you'd like it."

"Beer for me," said Reed. Berger sided him. Masters supplied them both.

"Now, tuck in. We'll give you about a quarter of an hour to blunt your appetites a bit. Then we'll talk."

"Right, Chief. Cheers!" Reed raised his glass.

The three women got into something of a huddle and discussed the outrageous prices of fuel. Masters and Green stood on the opposite side of the fireplace discussing the difficulties of lighting a pipe out of doors in a high wind. These dispositions had been made tacitly, so that the sergeants—as the only two eating— should not feel too much like the lions in the zoo at feeding time.

"Pipes are difficult," said Green. "I've seen some poor old blighters trying to light up, cupping the match in their hands, or inside their coats, backs to the wind and nothing worked. You need a convenient shop door for a pipe, whereas, with a fag, the merest flick of flame . . ."

". . . of electricity has gone up so much, I've deliberately cut down using half my things. And yet the bill always goes up and up for less and less. Bill says he's going to run-in on spurious charges every member of the Electricity Board he can find—and then perjure himself to make sure the charges stick. He's furious."

". . . very easy really. There are two ways. You fill the pipe and then put a bit of paper over the top. Big enough to come down the sides and hold in position with your left hand, taut, just like a drum skin. Then, like with your fags, you only need a flick of flame in the middle of the paper at the top of the bowl. It doesn't have to flame. It glows and burns outwards towards the rim. And if you draw on the pipe at the time, you get it going with no difficulty."

"And the second way?"

"Based on the principle that flames, like sparks, fly upwards. When you light a match and apply it to a pipe of baccy, you have to suck the flame downwards, against its natural inclination. This weakens the hold the flame has on the match stick. So if you

87

do it in a high wind which also blows the flame about—in a second direction—you weaken the hold completely and the match goes out. But if you pack the pipe and turn the bowl upside down, applying the match to the underside, the flame naturally travels up to the tobacco. When you draw on the pipe you help this process. So you strengthen the fire against any wind that's blowing, and you get your pipe going that much more successfully."

"I can see that," said Green. "You cup your hands round the flame and tuck the bowl in from the top. You can't do that if the pipe is the right way up."

"Right. And it looks as if the sergeants have about finished supper. I'll just offer them another beer . . ."

Reed handed a file cover to Masters. "I'll leave you to read all that for yourself, Chief. There's a lot of gup in it that I can't understand, but I've no doubt you'll make something of it."

Masters took it, glanced inside at the rather forbidding looking photostats it contained, and put it aside. "Any luck with the radio ham?"

Berger said: "I did that, Chief."

"Come on then, lad," said Green. "What happened?"

"I asked for details of code-name FPX923X, and after about three minutes I was told there was no such call sign allocated in Britain."

"They were sure?"

"The computer was. They're all there, both legal and illegal."

"Illegal?"

"There are some who transmit without the necessary authority. They're tracked down eventually, but I was told the Post Office isn't keen on deploying radio direction finders to locate some bloke who sounds off for a few minutes every now and again. The armed forces get fixes when they can and hand them over—for obvious reasons."

"Obvious reasons, Sergeant?" asked Bella. "Do you mean in case of clandestine activity by alien intelligence forces?"

"That's right, ma'am. Terrorist gangs, though, mostly. Alien intelligence forces use much more sophisticated methods of communication, usually."

"I see." So what you are saying is that in the face of danger, we are extremely lax in our precautions."

"Probably, Bella," said Green. "But let's not argue that one. We are not given either the resources or the authority these days to do what we'd like. Defence is an expensive word in the eyes of the politicians, and they'd rather risk having a grub at the heart of the rose than provide the money to buy a pest spray."

"Don't try to rebuke me, William. I believe in saying what I think should be said."

Green was unabashed. "And I'm not going to try and stop you. Say what you like, Bella, when you like, except when you start sidetracking an investigation. Let Sergeant Berger tell us what he knows, love, and after that we'll all join in a hymn of hate against all politicians."

Bella grinned. 'You know, William, you're rather good for me."

"Fine. Can we get on now?"

Bella inclined her head, and Berger continued. "They said there was something funny about that call sign."

"What?"

"The Post Office doesn't issue any with Fox as the initial letter. It's not one of the internationally agreed British allocations."

"So?"

"Well, I expected there'd be something funny about it, didn't I? If you and the Chief were asking about it, it would be for a good reason, like there being a bit of hanky panky connected with it."

"Brilliant thinking, lad."

"So I telexed Interpol. I got the duty Super to do it, of course. He wasn't very keen, but seeing it was the Chief asking . . ."

"You got what you wanted?"

"No. They said we should contact ITU in Geneva."

"And who are they when they're at home?"

"International Telecommunication Union. One of the Specialised Agencies of the UN. Among a lot of other things, they allocate each country its radio frequency spectrum and they register all radio frequency assignments. I looked them up. They're in the Place des Nations, Geneva. So I put a call through to their duty officer. He couldn't help much."

"How much?"

"Nothing, really, except . . ."

"Except what, for crying out loud?"

"Except that FPX is a call sign allocated by France."

There was a moment's silence, then Masters asked quietly, "Could the French authorities help you?"

"On a Saturday night, Chief? Have a heart!"

Masters turned to Green. "Did you happen to bring Prior's radio log with you?"

Green shook his head.

"I shall need it. If we call it a day now, the sergeants can call on Pulker first thing in the morning, borrow the key and get the book."

"You told young Sibbald you would get in touch with him."

"I'll do that. I don't see why we shouldn't take a drink off him as a small reward for services rendered."

Masters sat up in bed reading the file of papers Reed had brought him. Wanda lay alongside him, quietly, for almost twenty minutes before turning to him.

"George."

"Yes, my sweet?"

"A few hours ago, you said . . ."

He looked down at her. "I know exactly what I said. And what's more . . ." He dropped the papers on to the floor beside the bed. "And what's more I intend to keep my promise to myself." He put the light out.

"I thought it was a promise to me."

"It will involve both of us."

Half an hour later, as she was lying in his arms, she said quietly: "I thought I detected an air of satisfaction about you."

"Don't you always?"

"Mmm. But this time you definitely gave the impression that you were the cat that had got the cream."

He tightened his arm about her. "I am. You are the cream."

"George."

"Yes?"

"You know what I mean. You've hit upon something. Those papers. Did they help?"

"I should hate you to think that a glimmer of light shed by a file of texts would cause me to make love to you more enthusiastically than would otherwise have been the case."

"Silly chump! I didn't say that. Just that I sensed a feeling of elation."

"Not present normally?"

"The lily is always beautiful. Tonight you gilded it a little." Masters made a small sound of satisfaction.

"Here's the log, Chief. We had no difficulty getting it. That chap Pulker, though, is a bit of a talker. He wanted to know why we wanted it."

"What did you tell him?"

"What could I tell him? I haven't a clue what you want it for. Berger and I were discussing it on the way back, but unless you want to check the specific wording of some message, we couldn't see what you wanted it for."

Green and Masters were still at the breakfast table. Everything had been cleared away except two cups and the coffee pot. Green was reading the *Sunday Express* and drinking a very large cup of mahogany coloured coffee.

"Try time, son," he said without looking up from the leader page.

"Time?"

"Dates, lad, dates."

Reed glanced at Masters in bewilderment.

"The DCI is giving you a hint. He reckons you ought to have been on to what we want to check."

"Sorry, Chief, I'm not as fully informed as you are."

"Of course not. We'll put you in the picture." Masters turned the pages of the log until he found the entry where Prior had informed station FPX923X of his intention to marry. "The date on which he let the cat out of the bag is July the twelfth. Now, up till that date he had spoken to that station on an average of . . ." Masters turned back the leaves and scanned them ". . . at least twice a week, I would say." He turned back again. "But since that date, not at all apparently."

"Who did the calling?" asked Green. "Prior or FPX?"

Masters again consulted the book. Then he looked across at Green. "It would appear that FPX did, almost exclusively."

"But not since July the twelfth?"

"No. But we've got to appreciate that Prior didn't seem to have been on the air quite so much during those last few months."

"Other fish to fry," grunted Green. "He'd got Bella in tow, then. No longer the lonely widower whiling away the hours over his cat's whisker. But he did open up."

"Quite frequently."

"So it was FPX who was giving him the miss and not vice versa."

"It would seem so."

"You know so. FPX was keeping tabs on Prior, and as soon as they got to know he was getting married again they dropped him. Why? Because they'd got the information they wanted."

"Wanted?" asked Masters. "Or feared?"

"Feared," agreed Green. "Or at any rate it stung them into action."

Masters looked round. "Where's Berger? I want him to get on to the Yard to trace this FPX character."

"Your wife nobbled him," said Reed. "She wanted him to give her a hand with something in the garden. I think I heard something about sawing an unsafe branch off a tree."

Masters glowered. Green said: "After all, we are down here for a nice autumn weekend in the country."

"I'll get on to the Yard, Chief," said Reed. "That's if I can use the phone."

Masters nodded and Reed left them. Green lit a rather battered cigarette, leaned his elbows on the table and said: "There's a missing link, isn't there?"

Masters nodded.

"The bits you marked in those papers you showed me this morning fit in."

"I think so."

"But now we're up against it."

"In the time we have at our disposal. If we were on the job officially, we could ask questions in all sorts of places. But we're hamstrung, Greeny, because I really do not want the locals to get wind of what we're doing."

"Thereby getting the wrong impression."

"It would sour relations."

"And how! So what are you going to do?"

"There's only one thing I think I can do, and that's to use young Christopher Sibbald as a lever. If we feed him the right questions and make him demand the answers we might get things moving."

"What questions?"

Masters told him. At length. It took all of a quarter of an hour, and Reed had rejoined them long before Green had grunted his agreement to the plan.

"What about the call to Paris?"

"It's been made, Chief. The Yard is going to ring me back. They shouldn't be long. The Frogs have this sort of thing tied up tighter than we have."

"Maybe they do," said Green. "But they don't get quite so much caught in the knot as we do. The knot's tighter, but the bundle's smaller. Paris hasn't a clue about what goes on out in the sticks in France."

"Let's hope you're wrong about our Mister FPX."

It was another half hour before the call came. Reed took it. When he returned to Masters, Green said: "Well, son, what about it?"

"Evidently the Frogs are pretty hot on licences doled out to foreigners even if they're not very good about their own nationals. That X at the end indicates the holder of the licence is not French born. We don't make that distinction."

"Get on with it, lad. Cut the lecture."

"That licence is held by an Englishman named Gooding. Harry Gooding. Resident in Paris."

Masters said nothing. Green blew smoke rings.

"What's up, Chief? Have I said something wrong?" asked Reed.

"No, Sergeant. Just the opposite." Masters turned to Green. "We were morally certain, weren't we? But we should have known those messages came from an Englishman. They have that feel about them. Elsewhere in the log the English is correct, but too stilted."

"OK, OK!" said Green. "Be wise after the event. But we needed the name. Now we've got it."

"What's happening?" asked Reed. "I'm absolutely lost."

"The DCI will tell you," said Masters. "Get Berger. He'd better know, too." He turned to Green. "I'll phone Sibbald and arrange our lunchtime drink."

"Do that. But don't make it too late. I want to be back here for lunch. Bella's putting on wood-pigeon. One each in luscious gravy. I don't want to miss that."

Masters grinned and left them.

They were to meet Sibbald at The White Hart in Salisbury at midday. The three ladies stayed behind. Wanda had started a bonfire of leaves in the garden. Doris was helping her. Bella was about her household chores.

"Now," said Masters, as they arrived at the hotel. "For your sake, Reed, and yours, Berger, I will say that on no account must this case be mentioned directly to Sibbald. We are just four men —who happen to be cops—whom Sibbald has invited for a drink after meeting us in the presence of a legal colleague, Pulker. You may think I am being a bit mealy-mouthed about this, but I want to be able to say, in all honesty, that not a single one of us discussed the case of Regina versus Lunn with Sibbald. Is that clear?"

Both sergeants acknowledged the instruction.

Green said to them: "Sibbald knows the form. He won't try to trap you, so there's no need to be unnatural about it. Just tread warily. His nibs and I will be trying to give Sibbald an indirect nudge in the way we want him to go. He's an intelligent lad, as that business with the post-mortem report shows, so he'll catch on quick enough and co-operate."

They passed inside to the bar and found Sibbald waiting.

"What's it to be, gentlemen?"

The orders were given and Sibbald led them to a table in a dark corner of the bar. "I've more or less reserved this. If you'd like to occupy it, I'll bring the drinks over."

When they were all seated and Sibbald had been introduced to the sergeants, Masters asked the solicitor: "Have you, by any chance, ever encountered a material which is usually referred to by the initials PCPA?"

For a moment Sibbald stared and then a grin broke over his face. "As a matter of fact, I have, though when I came across it, it had a very lengthy chemical name which I would never attempt to pronounce."

"Do you happen to remember if you ever learned what it did? To what uses it was put? Or didn't you feel it necessary to investigate it at the time?"

The solicitor looked slightly shamefaced. Then he replied: "Do you know, Mr Masters, I think you could say I was guilty of taking things for granted at that time. I assumed the substance to be a drug."

"Go on."

"But I didn't take the trouble to confirm it."

"Perhaps there was no reason for you to do so."

"I certainly thought not. You see, the circumstances in which I encountered it were somewhat bizarre. It was found at post-mortem in the body of a man whom the pathologist declared had died of a heart attack. I saw no reason to question the cause of death and, therefore, supposed that the presence of a drug in the body was irrelevant."

"Why did you assume that?"

"Because the pathologist in question was an eminent man in his field and I suppose I trusted to him to mention the fact had the PCPA had any deleterious effect or had it in any way contributed to the death."

Green shook his head sadly. "These experts! One should never rely on them entirely. Don't misunderstand me. They're clever beggars, usually. But was this chap who did the post-mortem in question a forensic pathologist or a hospital pathologist?"

"A hospital man. But they're the same breed, surely? They're all knowledgeable doctors, accustomed to determining the causes of death. The only difference is that big centres of population can afford to keep one full-time for forensic investigations only, whereas in more sparsely populated areas like this, the hospital

95

man is called on to do work for the coroner and police in addition to his hospital duties."

"Quite, laddie. The forensic man is medico-legal, while the hospital man is medical only. The hospital chap spends his time determining the causes of death. The forensic man goes further. He investigates the causes of the causes, if you get my meaning."

"I think so. The pathologist we are talking about was asked to determine the cause of death in a certain case, and he did just that and no more. He established the man died of a heart attack and that was that."

"His finding was undoubtedly correct," said Masters.

"So why should I query it?"

"There is no suggestion from us that you should query that point," said Masters. "We are merely seeking information about PCPA."

"Then I'm afraid I cannot help you, at the moment. But I am very willing to try to find out whatever it is you would like to know. In fact, I can promise you I shall start asking questions tomorrow morning."

Masters shrugged. "That's very kind of you, but I'm afraid that would be a little late for our purposes. You see, we have to return to London tomorrow."

"Oh! In that case . . ." He took a diary and pen from his pocket. "Give me a few hints as to the line of enquiry I should pursue."

Masters leaned forward and spoke in a low voice. "My colleagues and I are of the impression that PCPA is a very rare drug, little used, because its actions in the human body are so numerous—and therefore unaccountable or unforeseeable—as to make it unethical for use in great quantities or on a regular basis.

"We should, therefore, be interested in knowing whether any general practitioner round here actually prescribes the drug, and if so, for what purpose. Our guess is that no GP does prescribe it. So if you should even hear that anybody is taking it, or has taken it, we should like to know, because we feel that potentially dangerous drugs should not be readily available and we should like to trace the sources of supply.

"Furthermore, from what little we know of PCPA, we understand that doses of two to four grams daily have been used, but that the higher dose rate can have serious side-effects. So if you, in the course of your enquiries, should ever come across a case where four or more grams daily appear to have been taken, we should be very interested indeed.

"And, of course, if ever you encounter a pathologist who discovers PCPA in a body and, after mentioning the fact, makes no further comment about it in his report, we should like you to ask why? Is it because, though capable of recognising its presence, he is unaware of its properties? We think the answer to this could be yes, because as we've said already, PCPA is little used and, therefore, is likely to be unfamiliar to a doctor. On the other hand, the doctor—or pathologist—in question may be aware of PCPA's beneficial properties in low doses, but not fully informed of its harmful effects, particularly in higher doses."

Sibbald said: "Could you go a bit slower please? I'm scribbling like mad, but I'm not keeping up."

"Sorry. I'll pause there. Ask me if you're not sure. In the meantime, we'll line up a few more drinks." He took out his wallet and handed Reed a note. "Same again all round, Sergeant, please."

As the new glasses were put on the table, Sibbald looked up from his task. "I think I've got it all so far."

"Good. Have a drink before we start again. Not that there's much more we'd like to know."

Sibbald grinned. "When I start asking questions on your behalf, am I going to cause a certain amount of consternation?"

"A bit, perhaps," said Green. "But remember, *we* are only curious. Other people may have a serious and specific reason to get to know about PCPA, so it would be just as well if your potential sources of information were to buff up on the subject. Who knows, you may be doing them a favour by giving them a bit of advance warning."

"I hope they see it in that light."

"Does it matter whether they do or not?"

Again Sibbald grinned, ruefully this time. "I suppose you know I'm out of my depth? When I was learning the trade in London, I just touched the fringes of all manner of legal work including the criminal stuff, and it seemed easy enough, or no more difficult than many other jobs. But that was years ago. Since I came down here I've done nothing more serious than motoring offences. This is the first time I've come head-on against the Crown in a really serious case. On my own, I mean. I'd never have embarrassed the prosecution with all these questions."

"You're talking out of turn," Green reminded him. "But don't worry, lad. When you instruct counsel and give him this sort of material to play with, you'll make a name for yourself. You'll find yourself busy on every circuit."

"Thanks. Sorry about mentioning you-know-what." He turned to Masters. "There was something else you wanted me to ask on your behalf, Mr Masters."

"Make a note to ask the general practitioner and the pathologist concerned in any case of ingestion of PCPA the state of the carcinoid syndrome in the body. No doubt their eyes will pop out, but basically, that is what PCPA has been used for."

"I don't even know what carcinoid syndrome is."

"Never mind. The quacks will. And they'll think you're very much on the ball. If there is no carcinoid syndrome, you can ask why PCPA was prescribed. If they say it wasn't, you've got the lead for asking what it was doing there and where it came from and so on and so on as we've already discussed. And that's the lot."

Sibbald closed his diary.

"Do you mind if I finish this drink and rush off? I have a lot to do in a short time."

"It's been nice to meet you, Mr Sibbald. Please remember us to Mr Pulker when you next meet him."

Sibbald got to his feet.

"Now this," said Green, "brings back memories." He slewed the small carcase of the wood-pigeon round on his plate to get it into a better tactical position for dismemberment. "My old mum used to bring these in on a great old meat dish. A deep one. She always poured her gravy over them before bringing them to the table. Good, thick gyppo it was, too, so that it disguised their shapes. That was how my old man liked it. Me, too. We used to tuck in." He took the leg off the small bird and gently levered the breast off one side. "I can't tell you, Bella, how I'm looking forward to this." He put a forkful in his mouth, moved his jaws a couple of times, savoured the flavour and then closed his eyes in ecstasy. "And to think," he murmured, mouth still full, "that in all the years we've been married, Doris has never once served this up to me."

"Have you ever asked her to?" asked Wanda.

Green opened his eyes. "Now don't you start ganging up on me, lass, otherwise I shall stop being your greatest admirer."

"That's a doubtful compliment."

"Huh?"

"You may be my greatest admirer, but it doesn't mean to say I stand highest in your admiration."

Green looked at her. "You're getting more like your old man every day. He's contaminating you. You're growing argumentative."

"That's no answer, and you know it."

"And I also know what you're trying to get me to say, so I'll say it. The one who gets my vote, every time, oddly enough, is the one who's never ever given me wood-pigeon for dinner in over twenty years. And that's an admission, because this little stock-dove is a real beauty." He fell silent and tackled his food once again.

"Now that the cameo is over," said Bella, "could you men tell us how the little matter of the freeing of Sid Lunn stands? Sergeant Reed, you're saying very little, but I feel certain you could furnish us with an account of what went on this morning."

"I could, Mrs Bartholomew. I will, in fact." He put his knife and fork down. "The Chief—Mr Masters—aided and abetted by Mr Green, conned a young and trusting solicitor into undertaking an investigation they felt unable to undertake themselves. It was beautifully done. They were asking the favour—on your behalf—and he was thanking them for asking him to do as tricky a bit of questioning among people who will resent it as I've encountered for some time. What is more, the young man almost had tears of gratitude in his eyes as he undertook to ask his questions today, Sunday, a day notoriously bad for questions to be welcomed by doctors and pathologists. The answers he would normally receive would be less than gracious. The answers he will get to the questions the Chief and Mr Green primed him to ask will be extremely tetchy. Why? Because, true to form, the Chief is setting a cat among pigeons. The questions will cause consternation, constituting, as they do, almost an accusation of negligence in certain quarters. It is a trick the Chief has. In the vernacular, it is known as 'stirring it'. He starts something to see what the reactions of various parties are. As I said, he is running true to form, and so, true to form, he should shortly solve your little difficulty."

They had listened in almost awed silence to this account. Then Bella laughed. "That," she said, "is what I suppose is meant by the brush-off. I'm to mind my own business and leave it to the professionals."

Masters grinned. "You asked for it, Bella. You tried to suborn by approaching Reed direct."

Reed said: "It's not only that, Chief. Quite honestly I'd have found great difficulty in giving Mrs Bartholomew a proper report because there's too much going on. And if I'd mentioned PCPA and she'd asked me what that meant I'd have been sunk, so I steered clear."

"Quite right, too," said Wanda. "And it was a beautiful speech."

"Almost as good as this wood-pigeon," said Green.

"Oh, you and your wood-pigeon," said his wife. "Anybody would think . . ."

She was interrupted by the sound of the telephone bell in the hall.

"I'll take it," said Masters. "It could be our friend Sibbald wanting to ask a supplementary question."

Masters gave the phone number.

"George?"

Masters recognised the voice. Anderson.

"Yes, sir."

"George, what the hell are you up to?"

"This and that, sir."

"This and that? You've set half of France alight. The Bureau is going bonkers."

"What about, sir?"

"You tell me. They've been on to me at home demanding to

know what you're doing and nobody here can tell them. Of course they don't believe us, that's why they got me. It's another case of Perfidious Albion as far as they're concerned."

"All I asked them was the name of the holder of a French ham-radio call sign. They gave it to me. A chap called Gooding."

"That's all?"

"That's all."

"Well, as I said, they're a suspicious crowd. As soon as the Yard starts asking questions about a British national resident in France and holder of a French radio call sign, they start wondering what it's all about. Particularly if we can't tell them—which they interpret as won't tell them. So they pootle round to this chap's apartment. And what do you think they found?"

"That the bird had flown. On his way to England."

"With the woman he lives with. But how the hell did you know, George?"

"Because Mrs Bartholomew's late fiancé's solicitor is expecting him to call at his office in Salisbury tomorrow morning."

"I see. George!"

"Yes, sir?"

"What are you up to? And what's all this about Mrs Bartholomew's late fiancé?"

"Very briefly, sir, Mrs Bartholomew was to have remarried this weekend. Unfortunately, some weeks ago her husband-to-be, a Mr Haydn Prior, died rather suddenly. His new will was to have become effective on his wedding day. But obviously, his former will now stands. All quite straightforward until yesterday, when a Mr Harry Gooding, resident in France, wrote to say he was Prior's illegitimate son, and he was proposing to contest the will. He announced he would call on Pulker—Prior's solicitor—on Monday to prove his claim. Pulker immediately called to inform Mrs Bartholomew, and found me here. He told me the story. It seemed a trifle fishy to me, so I started to make a few enquiries about Gooding."

"I should think so. Have you proved he's a false claimant?"

"To our satisfaction, yes, sir."

"It's a criminal offence, George, or could be."

"I realise that, sir. But in the course of our investigation, Green and I have uncovered something else we're not too happy about."

"It's your duty as police officers to clamp down on crime, George."

"We're not on our own patch, sir."

"What the hell does that matter? Report it to the locals."

"There's a snag to that, sir."

"What?"

"The slight—er—error, we have discovered, involves the local police."

"How?"

"They have a case which they consider watertight. So it is, on the surface. Anyhow, they're so satisfied they've got it dead to rights, they're refusing to dig deeper."

"And you've uncovered something which says they're wrong?"

"Yes, sir."

"What sort of a case is it, George?"

"Murder, sir."

Masters could hear the AC Crime whistle in dismay at the other end. Then—

"Now you've torn it, George. I'm not going to insult you by asking if you and Green are sure of your facts, but I do want to know if the locals know of your activities or involvement?"

"No, sir. But at this moment, a young solicitor, with whom we happened to have a chat in a pub earlier, is asking a few pertinent questions—in defence of his client, of course. We were careful not to discuss his case with him, knowing how sensitive the business could turn out to be, but you know how the young pick up hints from perfectly ordinary conversations . . ."

"George! You're acting the tit down there. You can't do it, do you hear? You've got to approach the locals and tell them what you know."

"How, sir? On what excuse?"

"Tell them you're an inquisitive, interfering busybody from the smoke, unable to keep his nose out of anything, and quite by chance you discovered some little fact . . . need I go on?"

"Tell them about Gooding, you mean, sir?"

"Yes. And do it now, George."

"Right, sir. Am I empowered to help them should they wish me to do so?"

"Yes, dammit, you are."

When Masters returned to the table, Green raised his eyebrows questioningly. Masters said: "Anderson."

Wanda said: "He's nice. A bit of a flirt. Every time I've met him he's made me feel very special."

Green grunted. "He's not your boss, otherwise you'd know different." He looked across at Masters. "And what did he want? As if I didn't know."

"Says we've got to get in touch with the locals."

"But how does he know what we're doing, Chief?"

"The French have been on to him. Evidently they make it their business to check up on foreign nationals if they are the subject of any external police enquiry."

"Sounds reasonable."

"They rang the Yard to ask what our interest was. Nobody there could tell them. They didn't believe that. Thought we were holding out on them. So they went higher."

"To Anderson."

"Quite. And he wasn't best pleased at being approached on a Sunday, particularly when he knew nothing about what was being asked. So he got on to me."

"Was he very cross, darling?" asked Wanda.

"So, so."

"Don't fret, love," said Green. "He'd pretend to be, but his blue-eyed boy can't put a foot wrong. I'll bet Anderson accepted every word George said as gospel, patted him on the head, verbally, and told him to carry on."

"More or less right," said Masters. "But the bit of news he was able to give me was that Gooding has already left Paris, accompanied by the young woman with whom he lives."

"News?" asked Green. "We could have guessed that."

"That he was on his way here, perhaps, but not that he has a woman in tow."

Bella said: "I can't believe that the fact that he has a mistress is relevant, George. Every man in France has one. A *petite amie*. It would be surprising if he hadn't."

Masters said: "I'll have some of the strawberry mousse, Bella, please."

"Good heavens, I was forgetting. Nobody has had any. Pass the plates, Wanda." As she served the mousse and handed it round, Bella continued her conversation with Masters. "I made an observation, George, and you tried to fob me off by reminding me that we hadn't had sweet. But it won't work. I demand to know why you think that the mistress of the man Gooding is important."

Masters was unabashed. "If Gooding has a mistress, it is highly probable that she is a party to his fraudulent attempt to get Prior's estate. His bringing her with him to England to make the claim goes some way towards substantiating that. Now, as investigators, we have to take into account all the possible characters in the play. For instance, something that might be impossible to achieve by one man, may be possible if he has an accomplice. Therefore, it is as well for us to be certain that there is an accomplice and to know the identity of that person. So, when we arrive at the stage where we need to theorise, we shall have all the dramatis personae in our minds. Because theories must fit facts and, as far as we are concerned, people are facts. So Gooding's mistress is another fact and we must allow for her, to try to define the part she has played, and to slot her neatly into her role."

"Specious," said his mother-in-law.

Doris Green said: "You're not suggesting George and Bill should overlook this woman, Bella?"

"Certainly not. What I'm saying is that they should not be diverted by the fact that she exists. If they do that they'll never get to the bottom of this affair. Concentration on vital facts is what's needed."

Green laughed aloud and handed his plate up to Bella. "Give us another spoonful of mousse, love, and stop being an old slave-driver."

"Bill!"

"It's right, Doris. Bella isn't satisfied with our progress. Or maybe she feels it won't be complete by the time we go home tomorrow. She's urging George on. That's admirable in its way. But she doesn't appreciate quite how far we've got in less than forty-eight hours. George—with the help of the rest of us—has uprooted a lot of trees. The layman won't appreciate that, perhaps. Bella obviously doesn't. She's got the whip out."

Bella handed him his plate back. "William, the trouble with this country is that everybody is prepared to travel at a snail's pace. You and George sat for hours over breakfast and then went out to drink before lunch. I would have thought that during those times you would all have been working on the case."

Berger, who had hitherto sat quietly, almost burst with indignation. "But that's not right," he expostulated. "The Chief and Mr Green were working very hard here after breakfast and in that pub before lunch. They were . . . were . . ."

"Yes, Mr Berger? They were what?"

"Putting together as sweet a bit of detection as you or anybody else could meet in a month of Sundays. The facts they're getting . . ."

"My point exactly, Mr Berger. Facts. Masses of them. But are they all valuable? I have a tidy mind. As I see it, you are amassing a great deal of information, all of it a hotch-potch, without design or apparent reason. None of it has, as yet, been fitted together so that we can begin to see a recognisable picture. Untidy, all of it."

"Don't you believe it, ma'am," replied Berger. "I'll bet the Chief could tell you right now exactly what happened."

"Why does he not tell us, then?"

"Because he has to have proof, ma'am. If he told you the story now, it would be just a yarn—fiction, if you like. But if he can get proof to show that every word he says is true, that every link has been thoroughly tested so that it will stand up to a battering in a court of law, then he has a case. And the Chief always has a case, otherwise he doesn't present it. That's why he hasn't presented it to you."

Bella replied: "My son-in-law has a truly loyal team. I am also assured by my daughter that his team has enjoyed some measure of success in the past. I am hoping for proof of it in this case."

"There you are then," said Green. "You're hoping for proof. That's just what the sergeant said. Don't get het up, Bella. At the outset, all you asked us to try and do was to get Sid Lunn off a murder charge. Your instinct was right. But you were working on a hunch. We've got to be sure. We will be, I promise."

"Very well, William, I'll accept that. Would you care to finish off the mousse?"

CHAPTER V

ALL OF THEM, except Bella, gathered in the sitting room after lunch. Wanda addressed them all. "I hope you'll forgive my mother. She obviously bore up very well at the time of Mr Prior's death. She kept it to herself—her grief at his illness and then the tragedy that night—bottled it up and didn't even let us know. But this weekend was to have seen her remarried and to have been a very happy occasion. As it is, she has kept going until she could unload all her doubts and unhappiness on to us, and now I suppose she is suffering from delayed shock. I've persuaded her to go for a rest."

Doris Green went across and put an arm round Wanda's shoulder. "Don't you dare apologise to us, lassie. There isn't one of us who has taken offence at anything your mother has said or done."

"That's right," said Green. "She's odd man out, you see, Wanda. Everybody else here is connected with the force. You and Doris by marriage only, of course, but at least you know how we operate. And I can sympathise with Bella. There is nobody on earth more maddening than your old man when he's on the job. I know because I've had a bellyful of it on numerous occasions. But that's the way he's made. He's lost if he's given a job that has to be done by the book. He won't wear the setting up of murder HQs and incident rooms full of clerks and ringing phones. So he's never given jobs like that. They're always given to blokes who can only work that way and, let's face it, some crimes can only be solved in that way. If Bella had seen that sort of thing going on, it would have appealed to her tidy mind. Everything noted and filed for cross-checking. Evidence of progress. But the way we play it—a sort of mental juggling act with every fact that comes to light—there's nothing to see. There's no play. Just an empty stage to look at until the final curtain comes down. And that's it. I tell you, love, if I had to watch us at work I'd go crackers and not just get a bit impatient like Bella did."

Berger said: "I shouldn't have said what I did, Mrs Masters. I'm sorry."

"Please don't be. My mother appreciates hard hitting. She'll have taken no offence, will she, George?"

"None whatever, I'd have said. She always gives me the impression that foolish ideas should be stamped on. And I don't think I need to say that her ideas were not foolish. You see, she doesn't know half of what we've done. None of the ladies does. But the other two . . ." he grinned at them, ". . . know better. They've experienced more of it."

Reed said: "I agree with Mrs Bartholomew."

"You what?"

"She'd have been right with every team at the Yard except ours."

"That's virtually what's just been said, lad."

"But she wasn't to know that, was she?"

"So what?"

"If she thought we were typical, Mrs Bartholomew would have a right to beef, because nobody else, carrying on the way we do, would ever deliver the goods. That's all. We're the exception that proves the rule."

"You've lost me, lad, and quite honestly, I don't know what we're rambling on about. I'm enjoying myself here, and Bella can say what she likes, when she likes, about me or anybody else if she lobs up wood-pigeon and strawberry mousse for Sunday dinner."

"Hear, hear," said Berger.

"Talking of which," continued Green. "After dinner on Sundays I like a bit of a kip . . ."

He was interrupted by the ringing of the phone.

"Oh, no! Just when I was about to put my feet up. Ten to one that's laughing-boy, Sibbald."

He was right. When Masters answered the phone the young solicitor said: "Mr Masters, I think you ought to know that Mr

Prior's doctor never prescribed PCPA for him. In fact he has never prescribed it for any patient at any time. He didn't even know what it was until he looked it up. When he heard there was evidence of a daily dose of six grams having been taken, he was very perturbed."

"Any carcinoid syndrome?"

"Nothing of the sort. Prior was as healthy as any man of his age. He was not being treated for anything before the business of not sleeping."

"Right. So there's a problem, isn't there. Did you manage to get the pathologist?"

"After a struggle."

"And?"

"And nothing. He says it is irrelevant in this case as it did not contribute towards the heart attack that was the cause of death. The shock of his wounds, fear and heavy exercise contributed to his death, but not PCPA."

"And he felt no need to comment on its presence?"

"Other than the fact that it was present, no."

"I see."

"So I've come to a dead-end."

"Have you? What about the police? Have you asked for information from them, yet?"

"Will it do any good? They'll consult the pathologist and I shall get the same answer as before."

"Maybe. But in that case you need your own medical expert."

"Do I?"

"You'll have to put somebody up to ask difficult questions. Somebody who knows his stuff. If you don't know anybody, consult your counsel. If he fails you, I might be able to help."

"How can you do that? You're treading on thin ice as it is, talking to me."

"Don't worry about that. The cat is out of the bag now. Over something which so far has not concerned you. I was only waiting to hear from you before getting in touch with the local police myself."

"Thank God for that."

"Don't count your chickens. They may tell me to mind my own

business. But what I want to know from you is the name of the officer in charge of the case."

"Detective Inspector Kennard."

"Where will I find him?"

"He's been working out of Amesbury."

"Right. If all goes well, I shall be calling on you officially or, alternatively, you will be able to approach me officially. Anyway, I shall let you know, so leave me both your home and office numbers."

Masters took the information down and a moment later thanked Sibbald for ringing and said goodbye. He returned to the sitting room.

"What?" asked Green, asprawl in an armchair, legs stuck out in front of him.

"GP not guilty and nervous. Pathologist uncooperative."

"Ah! As expected."

"DI Kennard of Amesbury has the case. I think I must now get in touch with him. Shall you want to come with me, if he invites me over, or would you prefer to stay and snooze?"

"I've a choice?"

"Of course. We're on leave. I've stumbled on something. Nothing more than that."

"Is that how you'd prefer to play it?"

"No. I'd rather have you with me."

"Then I'll come."

"Thanks. I'll see what I can arrange." Masters left the room to phone once more.

The station sergeant told Masters that DI Kennard was not in the station.

"Try to find him for me, please. This is quite urgent."

"You did say you were a Superintendent from the Yard, sir?"

"Yes I did."

"Can you prove your identity, sir? Before I disturb the DI that is?"

"Over the phone? I'm about to give you Mrs Bartholomew's number in Winterbourne Cardinal to ring. Check that back through your constable here, if you like. But don't keep me waiting more than five minutes, sergeant."

"Five minutes, sir? I might not get the DI for hours."

"Nevertheless, inside five minutes I want a progress report on your efforts to find him—just to show me that not everybody is taking a Sunday siesta."

Masters imagined he could hear the station sergeant grinding his teeth at the thought of some cocky bastard from the Met coming down here and throwing his weight about. But Masters felt he needed to use that weight. The sergeant had to live with Kennard all the year. The ructions there might be from a mild-mannered officer from the Yard, just passing through, as it were, would be as nothing to those from Kennard who, almost certainly, had a standing order that his Sunday afternoons were not to be interrupted. Not for anybody or anything except perhaps the landing and capture of a UFO complete with crew.

So Masters let it be known he was prepared to be the equivalent of a UFO. The sergeant could have the choice between bug-eyed monsters and DI Kennard.

The phone rang, not inside the five minutes stipulated by Masters, but sufficiently promptly for him to be gratified at the speed he had managed to engender in the local force.

"Masters."

"Superintendent Masters?"

"Right. Who's speaking?"

"DI Kennard. My sergeant said you wished to speak to me, Mr Masters. He said the matter was quite urgent."

"So it is, Mr Kennard. But it's your parish, not mine. I'm leaving here tomorrow, so I want to talk to you about it. I have Detective Chief Inspector Green here with me. When and where can we call on you?"

"Can you tell me what it's about, Mr Masters?"

"I prefer not to, over the phone. As I say, I'm in a delicate position here. I happen to have stumbled on something which is your business. I don't want you or your superior officers to think I am poking my nose into your affairs. So I wish to make a report. A verbal one. So how soon can you see me?"

There was silence at the other end of the line for a few moments. Masters knew he had bowled Kennard a fast one and the local man was wondering exactly how to play it. In Kennard's place he, Masters, would have stalled until such time as he could have mustered reinforcements in the shape of the most senior officer available at the time. To tangle with Scotland Yard brass must be a daunting prospect to junior local officers. Kennard would be making up his mind whether to conduct an opening skirmish alone, or to concentrate the full possible strength in time and space.

He evidently decided on the latter course.

"Perhaps I could give you and Mr Green a cup of tea while we talk, Mr Masters. Would half past four at my home suit you?"

"Fine. Give me your address and instructions for finding you."

Kennard had allowed himself well over the hour in which to locate somebody to side him. When Masters told Green of the arrangements, the DCI said: "Suits us, doesn't it? Saves telling everything twice. And it gives me time to have a few minutes' kip." He stretched his legs and put his hands behind his head. "The ladies have disappeared. Your lass is showing Doris something of the village. They asked me to say they'll see you when they see you, and to say that supper is cold tonight so it'll be a movable feast, leaving us free to come and go as we like without putting anybody out."

"Where are Reed and Berger?"

"Out back. In the garden. Wanda asked them to make sure the bonfire was safe to be left unattended. I reckon they'll be standing beside it chewing the fat."

"Thanks. I'll warn them we're going in about half an hour. I think it wiser to keep them hidden for the moment."

"Aye! No need to let them know we've deployed the whole team. It wouldn't look good with the yarn you're going to spin." Green closed his eyes to signify the talking had come to an end.

DI Kennard had been lucky. He had managed to locate Chief Superintendent Colegrave who, on hearing that two members of the Yard were nosing about in his manor, had made no bones about being present at the meeting Kennard had arranged.

Masters found the house easily enough. It was an undistinguished semi which, though in obvious good order, suggested —perhaps by the less than meticulously neat front garden—that the man of the house had little time to spare for domestic duties. As they pulled up at the gate, a large man, standing in the bay window and holding the nylon screen aside, moved out of sight. By the time Masters and Green were half-way towards the front door, the watcher had opened it.

"Mr Masters and Mr Green?"

"Yes. You are DI Kennard?"

"Come in, gentlemen. I took the liberty of informing Chief Superintendent Colegrave of your visit, and he said he would like to be present."

"Excellent," said Masters. "I would have had to make my number with him anyway . . ." They followed Kennard into the sitting room of the house, and the introductions were repeated. Kennard was big and bulky. In no way did he approach Masters' vast height, but he probably weighed almost as much. Colegrave was of smaller build and older. It struck Masters that away from London, where life is less hectic, policemen reached the higher ranks somewhat later in life than their counterparts in the metropolis.

Masters got the impression that Colegrave was somewhat guarded in his greeting. It was understandable. This wasn't being done by the book and one of the parties was from the Yard. It affected Kennard, too. He would take very little pushing to become overtly resentful. Masters judged it was time for a little soft soap, to grease the ways before getting down to cases. Green seemed to divine his thoughts, and set out to be affable in his own heavy-handed way.

"Sorry to disturb your Sunday afternoon snooze, Mr Colegrave. I wanted to put my feet up myself, but His Nibs here said no. Duty first. Kip second. And you, Mr Kennard! A day off in the bosom, as they say, and here's us to interrupt it."

"You told Kennard you wished to make a report," said Colegrave to Masters. "Almost as private citizens, he said, seeing you're not on a case down here?"

"I'd like to tell you about it."

Colegrave nodded. "We'd best sit down."

"First, let me apologise. As you say, we are not on a case. In fact, we're down here with our wives for a weekend in the country.

Nothing was further from our minds when we arrived . . ."

"Where?"

"In Winterbourne Cardinal. My wife's mother has a home there."

Colegrave nodded again. Masters thought he was going to be heavy going.

"Mrs Bartholomew?"

"You know her?"

"No. Only that she was to have married Mr Haydn Prior."

"Ah! The wedding was to have been this weekend. We didn't know."

"You what?"

"They had kept it quiet. We had been invited down here—some time ago—ostensibly for a weekend in the country. It appears that we were cast in different roles. My wife was to attend her mother and I was to have given her away. The DI would have sided Prior. The three of us, with Mrs Green, would have been the only witnesses."

"I see." The disbelief was still there in Colegrave's voice. "So you got down here when?"

"Friday teatime. It was then that Mrs Bartholomew told us of Prior's death and her intention of marrying him had he not died."

"If she'd been so keen on keeping quiet before, why did she tell you on Friday?"

"For two reasons. First, she had endured the death of her fiancé in silence. She had bottled up her emotions. But when we arrived, she obviously felt the need to confide in her daughter."

"She's suffering from a bit of delayed shock," supplied Green. "We had to put her to bed this afternoon because she was a bit het up."

"And the second reason?"

"Shortly after our arrival," continued Masters, "a solicitor called Pulker rang Mrs Bartholomew."

"Pulker of Salisbury? Haydn Prior's man?"

Masters inclined his head.

"He's not Mrs Bartholomew's solicitor."

"Quite. That is why the call was so strange."

"What did he have to say?"

"Before I answer that, I think I'd better explain that Prior had instructed Pulker to draw up a new will, in favour of Mrs Bartholomew, to become effective at the time of their marriage."

"Prior's death cancelled it?"

"Quite. But Pulker did Mrs Bartholomew the courtesy of calling on her after Prior's death to explain the circumstances."

"So what did he want on Friday night?"

"Prior's estate had been willed to various scientific institutions."

"We know," said Kennard. "I asked to see the will—just as a matter of routine."

Masters paused a moment in case Kennard had anything to add. Then he continued. "On Friday, Pulker was informed by a man called Gooding, who lives in Paris . . ."

"An Englishman?"

"So I believe. Gooding announced his intention of calling on Pulker tomorrow—Monday, that is. His intention apparently is to contest Prior's will on the grounds that he, Gooding, is Prior's illegitimate son."

Colegrave sat up at this revelation.

"Is it a genuine claim?"

"He sent Pulker a photostat of a birth certificate on which the father of the then unmarried Nurse Gooding's son was registered as a lecturer at Cambridge named Haydn Prior."

"That's good enough then," said Kennard. "This by-blow of Prior's can contest the will with, I'd have said, a chance of getting a bit of something."

"Hold your horses, laddie," counselled Green. "Hear it out, first."

"Hear what out?"

"Simply," said Masters, "that Prior was physically incapable of fathering a child."

"You mean he had no kids by his wife," said Colegrave.

"No, sir. Not just that. Because he and his wife wanted children they had tests done to discover what the trouble was—after trying for several years."

"Go on."

"Mrs Prior was found to be capable of bearing children, but

Prior was found to be incapable of impregnating her."

"Impotent?"

"No. Infertile. It's not the same thing."

"The tests were reliable?"

"Carried out in Addenbrooke's, Cambridge, by the leading men in the field."

Colegrave grimaced. "Who knew about him being infertile?"

"Mrs Bartholomew. She was his fiancée. They are mature people. They discussed these things."

"Not Pulker?"

"No. He merely rang up Mrs Bartholomew—again out of courtesy—to inform her of this unexpected turn of events. True, she had not yet married Prior, but they were engaged, and naturally she would want his last wishes to be carried out."

"Quite right, too," said Colegrave, thawing a little. "So your mother-in-law, seeing you were there . . .?"

"That's how it was, sir. Her daughter and I are her only family. She turned to us in her distress at this piece of news. So Green and I naturally did what we could. After all, it seemed as though some crime might be contemplated."

"Did you tell Pulker about Prior's infertility?"

"Yes, indeed. In fact, he called on Mrs Bartholomew to discuss what had become for him quite a serious problem. Meanwhile Green and I have been checking a few items. Our sergeants were in London and it was easy to get in touch with them."

"What have you discovered?"

"That Prior was without a doubt incapable of fathering children and . . ."

"And what?"

"That the name of the nurse assisting the doctor who carried out the tests on him was Gooding."

Kennard said: "The man's mother?"

"We assume so. We haven't traced her, but it would be too great a coincidence . . . wouldn't it?"

"Course it would," said Colegrave. "So that's it? That's what you came to report?"

"Not quite all," confessed Masters. "We thought we had better try and get a line on this Gooding chap."

"Any luck?"

"Yes. Mind you, Mr Colegrave, we only got down here forty-eight hours ago . . ."

"Well, you wouldn't get much in that time."

"I was thinking more of the fact that we haven't had much opportunity to consult you about all this before now."

"Forget that. What about Gooding?"

"We were taken by Pulker to see over Brooksbank, Prior's house, yesterday afternoon."

"Don't tell me you discovered something there."

"As a matter of fact, we did, by chance. Prior was a ham radio enthusiast. We saw his log there and glanced through it. We saw he had been in touch with a French call sign." Masters spread his hands. "You know how it is. France crops up once and then suddenly, there it is again. So just in case, we got in touch with the sergeants and asked them to check the identity of the owner of the call sign."

"Don't tell me it was Gooding!"

Masters nodded. "The same."

"So what are you suggesting, Mr Masters?"

"Nothing. The Assistant Commissioner and I had a talk over the phone this afternoon and we decided I should approach you and give you these facts. We knew it looked as if I'd gone behind your backs . . ."

Colegrave waved him to silence. "That doesn't matter. But . . . the Assistant Commissioner? That's flying high, isn't it?"

"Not in this case, sir, because the French are involved."

"How?"

"Evidently they begin to wonder what's on if foreign police start asking questions about foreign nationals to whom they—the French, that is—have issued ham radio permits."

Colegrave rubbed his nose with one finger. "Understandable, I suppose."

"So they asked the Assistant Commissioner what was the reason for our question about Gooding, and I had to tell him. So what started out as me giving my mother-in-law a bit of a helping hand was becoming a minor international incident. That being the case, we thought we'd better come to you straight away, even though it is Sunday, rather than wait until tomorrow."

"I get that. But what do you expect us to do about it? This false claim is important to you as a family matter, and to Pulker, but if Gooding has a birth certificate saying Prior was his father, he's free to contest the will. He can claim he honestly believed what was on the certificate. I know I believe what's on my birth certificate."

"Agreed," said Masters. "But I'd like to sort it out—for my wife's mother's sake. And that means operating in your area."

Colegrave rubbed his nose again while he considered this point. "You've got permission from the Met to stay here and sort it?"

"I was ordered to. The French will want an answer."

"Well, we have no objection, have we Kennard?"

"No, sir. Not if you say so."

"That is kind of you. But if we dig a bit further and turn anything up, what then?"

"By anything, you mean something that really would concern us?"

"Yes."

"Are you likely to?"

"Could be," said Green. "Something about this Gooding business stinks."

Colegrave made up his mind. "In that case it becomes our business. And as you're going to be here, I suggest we co-operate in exactly the same way as we would if we'd called you in—instead of you stumbling in as you have."

"We'll be very happy to do that, sir. You would like me to report to you?"

"Report to me and do something for Kennard."

"Any little thing we can do for your DI . . ."

"Anything specific?" asked Green.

"There's nothing I want," said Kennard forcefully. "Nothing I can't sort for myself."

"Excellent," said Masters, "but if, while we're here . . ."

"There is something," said Colegrave. "And this business of yours impinges on it."

"In what way, sir?"

"You know Mr Haydn Prior was murdered?"

"We've heard that, and also how commendably quick you were to arrest a poacher and charge him."

"Quick is right."

"Ah! Is there some snag?"

"On the face of it, no. Lunn, the poacher, was caught red-handed, still holding the gun with which Prior had been shot. He was bending over the corpse with his hand inside the jacket."

"Was he now?" asked Green. "Robbery?"

"That's our view. But Lunn claims he was feeling the heart. Prior's wallet was intact."

"No positive proof of robbery, then. But do you need it? The man died after being shot. You have the man who shot him. Murder."

"True enough. But he died of a heart attack."

"Consequent upon his wounds," claimed Kennard. "It's still murder."

"So it is, lad," agreed Colegrave. "Technically. But I've got my doubts."

"You think it was too easy, sir?"

"Not that. There's a lot of strong local feeling about it. Lunn was well known as a man who wouldn't hurt anybody."

"He shot rabbits and things," said Green.

"So he did. Nobody denies that. But everybody swears he would never harm a fly, let alone shoot a man."

"He was poaching," said Masters. "Poaching is theft. Lunn shot a man while engaged in theft."

"I'm not so sure about the theft bit," said Colegrave.

"No?"

"He hadn't got permission to shoot in that spinney," claimed Kennard.

Colegrave said: "True enough. But Lunn had been poaching those spinneys for years. Everybody knew that, including the land-owners. And they'd never complained to us or tried to stop him."

"You mean he could claim tacit consent?"

"I do. His counsel will claim it, too, and I'm not so sure that the landowners in question won't appear for the defence to back up the claim."

"He only ever shot by night," argued Kennard. "That shows he knew he was in the wrong and was trying to avoid detection."

"That's true," said Colegrave, "but local opinion says he just poached by night so as not to embarrass the landowners. If they saw him doing it by day, they'd have to forbid it, otherwise they'd have whole posses shooting their ground every day. But that sort don't go out by night. So Lunn just carried on. Besides, he had his job to do by day."

"But the magistrates remanded him?"

"On the evidence we produced. He reserved his defence. As Kennard maintains, on the face of it, it's an open and shut case. But when it comes to Crown Court and there's a defence put up . . . well, I'm far from sure that a jury will bring in a verdict of murder."

"Manslaughter?"

"I reckon Lunn would even contest that. We can only really offer to reduce the charge if he agrees to plead guilty to the lesser one."

Masters turned to Kennard. "You prefer to go ahead?"

"I do. We've got the case. If the jury acquits him, that's their business."

"And you, sir?"

"Naturally I want to proceed against a murderer. But I wondered if, as you're here, dealing with this business that involves Prior . . ."

"His estate, only."

"Right. His estate. But there is a connection. I'd like you to look at what Kennard's got. You're used to preparing cases like this. See if there's something we ought to do to strengthen our hand. Something we've overlooked."

"And if we can't find anything?"

"Give us your opinion. In other words, tell us if we've got a case or we haven't. Will you do that?"

"With pleasure. Does Mr Kennard agree?"

"Of course he does, don't you, Kennard? He's like all cops. He likes a successful case. But he doesn't want a flop if he can avoid it. He'll be a bit brassed-off if you pull his stuff to bits, but in the long run he'll be grateful."

"I'll get the tea," said Kennard. "The missus has got a tray ready."

"Good lad," said Green. "Do you want a hand to help carry it?"

Kennard declined. He was not in the best of humours. He had returned and was pouring tea and handing round wedges of Victoria sponge when Masters said, "Oh, by the way, sir. My sergeants had to come down to bring some important papers. As we weren't likely to be back at the Yard tomorrow they brought the file down. They're in Winterbourne Cardinal now. I think I'd better ask them to hang on. Just until we see what the form is."

"Good idea. Important papers?"

"The drug business. I'd started something we never finished, and then when Reed called into the office to do those errands for me he was collared and told to get the paperwork to me."

"I see. The whole team's on leave is it?"

"Not so's you'd notice," said Green. "We hadn't bargained for this little lot when we set out on Friday."

"My domestic problems," said Masters with a shrug. "Now, when shall we get down to discussing your problem, Mr Kennard?"

"Your old man," said Green to Wanda, when they had returned to Bella's home, "is as big a liar as I've come across, and believe you me I've met some."

"Don't listen to him, darling," said Masters as he kissed his wife. "I merely practised a little verbal subterfuge."

"Oh, but I will listen. What happened, Bill?"

"He conned a pair of perfectly respectable rozzers."

"I told no deliberate lies."

"What's the difference between a lie and a deliberate lie?"

Masters, his arm round Wanda, smiled at her. "Suppression of the whole truth or presentation of half the truth."

"A half truth."

"No, no. Half of the truth. A half truth suggests I mixed sugar with sand. What Bill means is that I told our local colleagues—for instance—nothing about having seen Sibbald and the PM report or PCPA."

"That's not what I meant," retorted Green. "You led an unsuspecting Chief Super to believe that Reed and Berger came down here to bring you a file of important papers."

"The truth."

"Just. But you allowed him to think they had to do with a different case."

"I mentioned drugs. PCPA is a drug."

"We know that. He doesn't. And you didn't tell him you had instructed those two to bring the papers down. You let him think it was fortuitous that we are all down here."

"If he jumped to that conclusion . . ."

Green turned to Wanda. "You want to watch him. He's as slippery as an eel."

"Did you manage to do what you set out to do?" she asked. "To get yourselves signed on without hurting any feelings?"

"I've just told you. Thanks to your old man's superb technique in leading people astray, they were almost begging us to step in before we left."

She smiled at him and tossed her head. "That's all right then, isn't it?"

Green grinned back. "Everything's all right when you smile, lass. Now, where's my old lady?"

"I think she's dozed off in front of the fire in the sitting room."

"And the sergeants?" asked her husband.

"They got their shoes muddy so they've gone into the kitchen to clean them. They're cleaning a pair of mine, too. Isn't it nice of them?"

They went into the sitting room, which was only half lit by a single reading lamp and the glow of the fire. Doris stirred as they entered. Green went over to her and kissed her forehead.

"Is that you, Bill?"

"Who did you think it was? The milkman?"

"Silly ass. My, but you're cold."

"A drink, I think," said Masters. "Who's for what?"

The sergeants joined them a few minutes later. "What's on, Chief?"

"Help yourselves to a drink and we'll talk."

"What you've got to remember, lads," Green said to Reed and

Berger, "is that we know a lot more than we've let on we know. To give us a break, His Nibs here had the nous to ask Kennard if we could glance through the Lunn file, so that we could discuss it between ourselves this evening. He came to the Amesbury nick with us, and we made a few notes—or pretended to. But the point is, the PM report was there. So nobody can now ask where we got the information about PCPA from. But everything we know about its properties has had to be learned tonight. Savvy?"

"Over the phone, from the Yard?"

"Right."

"So what do we do now?"

Green turned to Masters, offering him the question to answer.

"I think the two most pressing things are . . ."

"Yes?"

"To have supper and to review our situation."

Over the cold ham and pickles, they talked.

"We're officially in, now," said Masters, "so we can take whatever steps we like. The locals have ignored the PCPA that was found in the body. We've got to alert them to that, and we've got to find how it got there. Then the second part of our job is to decide what to do about Gooding. Do we intervene tomorrow, or do we leave it to Pulker to deal with him, using the information we have provided?"

"It's the solicitor's job, Chief. To begin with at any rate. Pulker wants to shoot him down in flames and see him off." Berger made it sound simple.

"Does he?"

"You don't think so, Chief?"

"Use your loaf, laddie," said Green. "Gooding lives in France. If Pulker sends him away with a flea in his ear, he could return to Paris and then where are we if we want him for something else?"

"You mean he'd be out of our reach if we discovered he'd been involved in Prior's death?"

"That's it, boyo. Have you ever tried to extradite somebody?"

"So what do we do?" asked Reed. "Get Pulker to string him along for a day or two until we get the answer?"

"I really think that would be best," said Masters. "And as Gooding is due in Salisbury tomorrow, it means we have to brief Pulker fairly soon. I don't think we need to suggest what line Pulker should take. Solicitors are adept at stalling."

"The law's delays," said Wanda. "Have some more red cabbage, Doris. Ena Cully pickles it herself. I'm going to ask her if she's got a jar or two to spare for me to take home. Judging by the way George is wolfing it now, it will come in very handy."

"That's a good idea, dear. These men of ours come in at all hours and expect meals when they arrive. I make a point of keeping something cold up my sleeve for Bill. He loves corned beef, fortunately."

"Pulker will say, presumably, that he will need to check the original birth certificate?"

"That and quite a number of other things, I imagine. What I shall ask him to do is to promise to do everything necessary within the next few days if Gooding is willing to stay around."

"We'll have to see Gooding," said Green. "Not officially, of course. Just to identify him and to keep track of his movements."

Masters nodded. "I think Reed and Berger should have that particular chore. I wonder if Pulker could conceal one of them so that he could overhear the initial interview?"

"Maybe. There are lots of doors and rooms in that rabbit warren of his. It's worth trying to lay on."

"Right. We'll try and fix it. I can't see why Kennard can't be persuaded to provide a tape recorder and a camera. Reed, you can fix all that. One inside if possible. One outside with car and camera. I want mug shots."

"Right, Chief. Anything else?"

"Play it as it comes. Don't forget he has a woman in tow. If she's with him, I want shots of her, too. I want to know where they're staying—in Salisbury or London. Everything."

"There's Gooding's mother. We ought to trace her."

"We could get Pulker to ask for her address, if she's still alive and in this country."

"And her name," said Doris. "She will certainly have been married if she was as jiggly as that doctor said she was."

"Good point, love," said Green and winked at Masters. "Then what? Do you want me to see her?"

"If that's possible. If needs be, you can have my car. Wanda will drive you."

"That's OK by me," said Green.

Wanda said: "Doris and I had both better go with him if he's visiting nubile blondes, however elderly."

"Right. That's settled."

"What about you?" asked Green..

"I'll be all right. I can either borrow Bella's car for the day or scrounge one from Kennard."

"To do what?"

"I think I'd better hang around so that it doesn't look as if we were neglecting him altogether. A little lecture on the value of the forensic side of post-mortems, perhaps. A few suggestions concerning the things we have hammered out between us during the last two days."

"Concerning Lunn's attitude? How he would have slipped away if he'd not intended to help. That sort of thing?"

"I think it would do no harm to point out the value of basic thinking."

"Quite right. Now, let me see. Mincemeat tart or fresh fruit salad. Which shall I have a lot of?"

"Why not both?"

"That would be greedy. I don't want to make a pig of myself."

CHAPTER VI

MRS BARTHOLOMEW came down after dinner. She had had a tray in her room, but had determined to spend the evening with her guests.

"I owe a lot of apologies," she announced as she came into the sitting room. The four men, all on their feet at her entry, murmured vague words meaning that she was not to bother to apologise. But she, nevertheless, insisted on having her say.

"I brought you all down here under false pretences and then I castigated you for failing—as I thought—to be as unrelenting as you could have been in my cause. That was unforgivable of me. You would have every reason to leave me to stew in my own juice. That you have not done so is a measure of your kindness and, I believe, dedication to your profession."

"Not it," said Green. "We were about to leave you this afternoon, but our boss got to hear about our enquiries in France and rang to tell us to stay here until we got the job sorted. So we told the local police we're here to look into Gooding's false claim to Prior's estate and everything is now on an official footing. That being so, you'd better mind your p's and q's because everything you say will be . . ."

"Bill!" protested his wife. She turned to Bella. "He's pulling your leg."

"I hope not, Doris. I hope William meant that everything I say will be duly noted and acted upon."

"He did," said Masters. "And what is more, he and I are about to go about your business now."

"Now?" asked Green.

"To see Pulker, and to get the tape recorder if we can. And I thought we might try to get in touch with Sibbald, too."

"Do you want us, Chief?" asked Reed.

"You and Berger can keep the ladies company. We'll be back as soon as we can."

Pulker was pathetically grateful to see them. He was wearing slacks, a sweater and slippers and had been watching television. Alongside his chair, on a coffee table, was a plate that had obviously held his evening meal, which had equally obviously been eaten on his knees before the box. A Ruddles empty bottle and a dreg-stained tumbler showed his choice of beverage to wash down the food which, from the slight remains on the plate, seemed to have been something containing tomato sauce. Green guessed at beans. Masters at some form of pasta.

The solicitor switched off the television, and after ushering them into his sitting room, hurried across to collect the dirty crockery. He seemed a little shamefaced that they should have caught him off-parade, and he murmured the information that his woman didn't come in at weekends and so he had to fend for himself.

"Don't worry, Geoff," said Green. "We've all had to batch for ourselves at some time. And a right mess we've made of it, I can tell you. I remember once when Doris was away for a fortnight I thought I'd be clever and do my washing before she got back. There were no laundrettes in those days and I wore woollen socks when I was on the beat. What I did was fill the bath with cold water and put a couple of dozen pairs in to soak. I thought they'd be easier to wash next day. I didn't know you shouldn't soak wool like that. They came out small enough to fit pigmies. Shrunk to glory, they were. It took me some time to live that down, I can tell you."

Pulker smiled. Green had achieved his object. The lonely solicitor began to remember his duties as host, and more bottles of Ruddles were brought in.

"Tape recorder?" asked Pulker, as Masters briefed him. "I've never had occasion to use one of those. I'm not certain that I could operate one clandestinely. I make notes, you know. On large sheets of paper in soft pencil. Won't that be enough for your purpose?"

"I would rather like to get to know the type of man Gooding is. Notes made by you, however comprehensive, won't give me as much an indication of his character as would his evasions, tone of voice and general attitude."

"I see. What a pity you can't actually be present."

"Perhaps Bill could be. Not actually in your office, of course, but just outside it, with the door ajar."

"In the dressing room perhaps? Perhaps you don't remember . . ."

"I do. Your office is, in fact, one of the bedrooms of the original house. There is another door . . ."

"Into what we still call the dressing room." He looked across at Green. "It is used nowadays as our rather primitive kitchen. We have a gas ring and a kettle in there and the girls brew our drinks."

"Suits me," said Green.

"Bill has a very good memory," said Masters. "Long years of constant practice have made it remarkably reliable. If he could be there, he would get what we want to know."

"I would prefer that."

"Right. Now one last question which you must put to Gooding. On no account must you forget to do so."

"What is it?"

"Ask him how he got to know that you were Prior's solicitor."

"Good heavens! I'd never thought of that. Is it important to know?"

"Come on now, Geoff," said Green, setting down his empty glass. "How would you find out who was somebody's solicitor in Paris or Edinburgh or wherever? Short of asking the chap concerned, that is?"

"Dear me! I really can't answer that, as I have never had to undertake such a search. Perhaps I should be obliged to employ a private detective agency in the area concerned. For them the matter would be quite easy to resolve, I imagine."

"Quite. In other words, you'd have an agent in the area—however temporary. George wants to know if Gooding had an agent, too."

"An accomplice, you mean?"

"It's a possibility. You never can tell with bees, and it strikes me Gooding could be a bit of a bee."

"To be sure," said Pulker, smiling. "Is that all?"

"I think so," said Masters. "Make it comprehensive. Try to find out what he does for a living. Why he lives in France. Who he lives with. And so on."

"I shall do my best."

"I'm sure you will."

"And stall him," reiterated Green. "We don't want him scarpering back to France. Be as nice as pie to him, so's he'll not suspect anything, but explain that you must satisfy yourself as to the authenticity of his birth certificate and that it will take you a day or two."

"Shall I make another appointment for him to come and see me on, say, Wednesday afternoon?"

"Why not? Say that you will be in a position to let him know whether you and your fellow executor will be prepared not to oppose his application or whether you will have decided to fight it tooth and nail. Your decision will be important to him."

"What if he jibs at the idea of waiting? He might think we will fight him whatever happens."

"You've got to be clever," said Masters. "Don't actually say so, but hint at the fact that your fellow executor is an important man who would far rather reach an accommodation over this than have it dragged through the courts to become a *cause célèbre*. I'm certain that is true, if I'm any judge of what I heard over the phone last night. So make sure he understands that all will be by no means lost if he stays. Should he still insist on going, after that, let him know that you would certainly regard his claim as spurious if he is not prepared to stay and work the thing out amicably."

"Oh, dear," said Pulker, "I'm sure you would do this so much better than I shall."

"Not so," replied Masters. "We have our methods of conducting interviews—police methods. They would certainly frighten him, however much we tried to disguise them. But you are the genuine article. A little flustered, maybe, but what solicitor would not be flustered by the appearance of a claimant to a huge fortune, the disposal of which, before he intervened, had seemed completely straightforward? Tell him so if you wish. It will do no harm to let him think for a time that he is dealing with somebody not quite up to his mark in double dealing."

"You are painting him as a blackguard. We're not sure he is."

"That remark," said Green, "illustrates George's point. As policemen we would regard him as a villain. You don't, necessarily. That feeling would come through in an interview."

"But why regard him as anything other than a genuine claimant?"

"For the simple reason that he did not make himself known during the lifetime of the man he says was his father."

"Maybe he felt Prior wouldn't want to know."

"He couldn't tell that till he'd tried. And he must have realised that even Prior couldn't blink facts. If Gooding was his little bastion of society, Prior could not have denied it. At least this claim would have been authenticated. But George and I, being suspicious blokes, reckon Gooding steered clear while Prior was alive because Prior was—or so Gooding believes—the one man who could have denied the claim."

"Could he?" asked Masters. "Oh, I know he could have denied it, but obviously Gooding didn't know of Prior's inability to father a child. What would one of us do—or any normal man for that matter—if years after a child had been born, the mother were to appear and say we had sired it? Particularly if she'd put our name on a birth certificate? And please don't say blood tests. They are notoriously unreliable."

Green sucked at his partial denture. "It would, literally, be a bit of a bastard," he admitted.

"What about you, Mr Pulker, if you were so accused?"

Pulker spread his hands. "How could one deny it. Oh, I know one could. But if the mother or her child were to make a song and dance about it, a considerable amount of mud would stick."

"Quite so. We don't for the moment think that Nurse Gooding, thirty years ago, planned a clever crime. But we do think she was panicked into giving the name of a man as the child's father. The name she first thought of. But now we think that the child she bore then is now out to take advantage of what his mother did and we further think that his timing points to a carefully laid plot. In other words we think he is a villain."

Pulker grimaced. "I'm pleased you've told me, and I hope it helps me to get what we need out of him tomorrow."

"I have no doubt that it will." Masters got to his feet.

"Are you going? So soon?"

"I feel we should let Mr Sibbald know that we are now officially involved in the case. I promised him we would."

"Ring him from here," urged Pulker. "I'll find you his number."

The next morning, before nine thirty, Masters called on Kennard in the latter's office.

"You're alone?" asked the DI suspiciously.

"Entirely," replied Masters airily. Then relenting, knowing that Kennard would be anxious to know what the others were about, he said: "Mr Green is standing by at Pulker's office to get the address of Gooding's mother. When he has it he will try to interview her."

"Try?"

"If she lives within striking distance. London or the Midlands, say. If she's further away he'll have to play it as it comes."

"And the sergeants?"

"I have detailed them to keep an eye on Gooding himself. I'd like to know where he's staying, whether he's alone, who he talks to . . . all the usual."

"And you, Mr Masters?"

"May I sit down?" Masters indicated the visitor's chair which Kennard had not offered him. The DI nodded. Masters sat and took his pipe out of his pocket. He looked round the office. It was small, scarcely ten feet each way, but it had been decorated in a way which suggested that the local police authority was not responsible for the furbishing. The walls were papered in a colour which reminded Masters of strawberries crushed in ice cream. The window was curtained in pin-tucked drapes with a geometric pattern. The desk had all manner of clerical aids: perpetual calendar covered in brown leather, ash tray in green marble, silver ink stand, triptych blotter with green paper and red wings.

Kennard's desk chair boasted a cushion in gold draylon, and on the walls was a series of montage art, all of dried flowers and grasses mounted under clear plastic covers shrunk on to narrow boards. The brown floor covering was partially disguised by a rust and off-white rug, the twin of one Wanda had pointed out to Masters on a recent visit to Marks and Spencers.

"You live comfortably."

"Why not?"

"No reason that I know of. I take it that you brew your own coffee, rather than use canteen tea?"

"I have my own kettle, yes."

"Somehow I thought you would." Masters began to fill his pipe with Warlock Flake. "But to get down to business. Mr Green and I went to see Pulker last night, just to brief him on what we would like him to ask Gooding."

"Can Pulker do it? Get your information, I mean? He seems a bit wet to me."

"Have you had a lot to do with him?"

"Only the once, when I wanted to see Prior's will."

"Didn't he go round Brooksbank with you?"

"Brooksbank? Oh, Prior's house! We didn't have to visit it."

"I see."

Kennard shifted uneasily in his seat. "Look, Mr Masters, Prior was shot. We caught the man who shot him red-handed. There was no need to make a thing of it."

Masters lit his pipe. When it was drawing satisfactorily, he said: "I can see your point."

"There you are then."

"If you were satisfied that Lunn was your man."

"How do you mean?"

"Mr Kennard, to prepare a cast-iron case against Lunn, you have not only to satisfy yourself, but also a jury. In other words, once you were happy you had the right man, you should have gone over the whole business again making sure there were no loopholes."

"Lunn was caught red-handed."

"So you keep saying. But what would your answer be if defending counsel asked you why Prior was in that spinney in the early hours of the morning?"

"I don't have to know that."

"But you do, particularly if the defence can show that Prior had never before been known to be out and about in that area at that time of night."

"Why?"

"Counsel will suggest he went there for some purpose."

"How can they?"

"Can you argue that it is not strange for a highly intelligent, comparatively elderly man to be cavorting in a wood in the small hours?"

"No, I suppose not."

"How much of a step from there is it for counsel to suggest he must have had a reason for his presence there."

"What possible reason could there be?"

"You say he went there without a reason?"

Kennard grimaced. "What are you getting at?"

"Do highly intelligent men do what Prior did without reason? Answer yes or no."

"Yes."

"Do the judge and jury believe you? Can you substantiate it? In view of the fact that Prior had never done so before?"

"They should believe it. People do all sorts of odd things."

"So they do. But will your word be accepted if counsel can refute it by suggesting that Prior must have had a reason for his excursion? A nefarious purpose if you like."

"Nefarious? Such as?"

"What would you say if it was suggested Prior could have gone there to kill Lunn?"

"Ridiculous."

"Can you think of a better reason for a meeting between two men—that ends in the death of one of them—than a serious quarrel?"

"Quarrel, maybe. But it's unthinkable to suggest Prior could have gone there to kill Lunn."

"But is it not equally unthinkable to suggest that Lunn had gone there to kill Prior?"

"We're not suggesting premeditated murder."

"What sort of murder are you suggesting?"

"Unpremeditated."

"With no motive?"

"I don't have to prove a motive."

"True. But it helps with a jury."

"I don't know what went on between them."

"No evidence of bad blood or local feud?"

"No."

"So at twelve yards range Lunn blasts off at a man. There is no quarrel, no motive, no reason at all. Tell me why you think Lunn fired. The jury will want to know."

"He said he was frightened. Prior jumped out on him."

"So he fired?"

"So he says."

"Can you disprove that?"

"No, but he can't prove it, either."

"To win your case, there must be no shadow of doubt. You expect the jury to believe you. Why shouldn't they believe Lunn? Particularly as the opportunity to finish Prior off with another shot was not taken when it could have been had there been intention to kill."

"You say Lunn fired in self-protection?"

"I didn't say that. But it's a thought. His counsel may well toy with it. Unless he gives them something else to use."

"You mean the accidental discharge he says it was."

"Reflex action when frightened? Finger tightened on the trigger when Prior jumped him?"

"That's his story."

"You find it unacceptable?"

Kennard leaned back. "Look, Mr Masters, I don't have to find anything acceptable or unacceptable. Prior died as a result of gunshot wounds inflicted by Lunn. That's murder according to law, and there's no denying it."

Masters tapped his pipe out gently on the marble ashtray. Kennard watched him for a moment and then continued. "Even if a burglar breaks into your house you are guilty of murder if you kill him. Even provocation such as robbery is no excuse."

"Unless you can prove you felt threatened with physical injury or death yourself."

Kennard shrugged. "You'd have a hard job to get away with it if the burglar was totally unarmed. Prior was totally unarmed. A man in late middle-age. No physical threat at all to a wiry countryman like Lunn who, don't forget, *was* armed and, not only that, had a cartridge up the spout."

"Lunn would know Prior was unarmed?"

"That's immaterial."

"Perhaps. But you have to convince a jury. I would guess that every member of that jury would absolve a man who killed an intruder in his home. They don't believe in the minimum force clause. Very few do."

"You mean they'll be on Lunn's side?"

"Why not? He isn't a yobbo against whom there would be prejudice. He's a countryman who will be tried by countrymen. And there'll be a lot of evidence to show he's a kindly countryman. It will be all stacked against you."

"What you're saying is that we should drop the case?"

"Certainly not."

"What's all this about then?"

"I've been trying to show you that even if you accept that the case against Lunn is open and shut, you must investigate it fully so that it won't fail because you haven't prepared it properly. In other words, there is no such thing as an open and shut case. There has to be a full, rounded presentation of the prosecution, not just an assertion of what you believe—or even know—to be true."

Kennard sat back. "That's all very well, sir. But all you've given me is a lot of chat. No facts. Talk won't get me anywhere. I've no means of getting to know why Prior was in that wood, or why he jumped out on Lunn, if he did. Anyone can speculate."

"You're wrong," said Masters quietly. "You haven't even tried. If your efforts to solve this case were as great as the care you seem to lavish on your office, you'd find you could get just those answers."

Kennard flushed and set his jaw.

"Are you telling me I'm not doing my job, sir?"

"I'm certainly saying you haven't done this one yet. And don't try to go all hard on me, because it won't wash."

"Perhaps we should let Mr Colegrave decide that."

"That suits me fine. Shall we go together to see him now, if he's in? But I warn you, once we're in there, I shan't let you off the hook."

"Meaning?"

"I've only been down here since Friday evening, and I haven't had the advantage of your local knowledge and assistance, but in three minutes flat I could demolish your case against Lunn and prove—with facts, Mr Kennard—that you have made no attempt to prepare this case."

Kennard stared across at Masters, who proceeded slowly to re-fill his pipe. There was a long silence broken eventually by Masters who asked: "Well, shall we go to see Mr Colegrave or not? It's up to you."

Kennard did not reply. Masters gave him time to simmer down, then as he lit his pipe, he said: "If you were to make us a cup of your coffee, I could, of course, tell you all about it."

"Mr Gooding for you, Mr Pulker."

"Thank you, Fiona. Show him in please."

As his typist left, Pulker glanced across at the dressing room door to satisfy himself that it was ajar. Green had waited at the window until a taxi had arrived at the front door of the office.

"Is this him, Geoff?"

Pulker had looked out. "I don't know. But it is certainly not one of my clients. Nobody I've ever seen before."

"Then it's him. I'll hide."

When Fiona showed Gooding in, Pulker was busy with a pad of paper and pencil. Across the top he had written Haydn Prior Estate and Mr H. Gooding, with the date.

Pulker got to his feet. Gooding was a big, blond young man, with broad shoulders and squarish features. The impression he gave was that of impermanent good looks, destined to fade sooner than those of his less physically presentable brethren. Pulker remembered that his mother had been described as a nubile blonde in the days when she had given birth to him. What was she now? Faded? Blowsy?

"Good morning, Mr Gooding. Please sit down.

"May I take my coat off? It's a warm day for autumn."

The voice was good. Well modulated and musical.

"Are you staying in Salisbury?" asked Pulker, hanging the coat in his little wardrobe.

"In London."

"With your mother?"

"No. At a little place called the Vessan Hotel."

"I don't think I know it. But your mother . . . I asked about her because I shall obviously want to talk to her. Does she live with you in Paris?"

"No . . . she is Mrs Stringer. She lives with her husband, my step-father, that is, in Ryde."

"That's the Isle of Wight, isn't it?"

"They keep a boarding house there."

"I see." Pulker was making his notes as they talked. "Could I have the address, please, and the phone number if they have one."

The information was supplied quite readily. When he'd finished writing, Pulker put his pencil down and looked up.

"I'm afraid you've bowled us a fast one, Mr Gooding."

"My claim?"

"The fact that it came out of the blue. Totally unexpected. Totally. The settling of Mr Prior's affairs had seemed such a simple business before your . . . your bombshell."

"Does that mean that you accept the claim?"

"No, no, no. Even to suggest that would be to mislead you, Mr Gooding. Please understand the situation. You and I are . . . well, not exactly on opposite sides of the fence, but I am most definitely not your man of affairs. You must engage a solicitor to act on your behalf, if you have not already done so."

"To fight the claim for me, you mean?"

"To represent you legally."

"Isn't that the same thing?"

"Not necessarily. It may be that there will be no fight. That we shall not oppose you. But your interests must be properly safeguarded by an independent lawyer unless . . ."

"Unless what, Mr Pulker?"

"It suddenly occurred to me that perhaps you are a solicitor yourself—in industry maybe. A company lawyer working in the EEC?"

Gooding laughed. "I am an interpreter, Mr Pulker. And a translator. I work for a large company in Paris, and it is true that most of our work has come about because of the needs of the Common Market. But law . . . no. I have something of a flair for languages. Chiefly Italian, which I read at university, but I have built on my schoolboy French to a degree where I can work in that language quite comfortably. A three-way ability in translation and interpretation is an asset. Particularly as, being in contact with it so much, I can even manage a smattering of Flemish and a little German."

"You must be a very accomplished young man. You are kept busy?"

"The agency is a flourishing business."

"What sort of thing do you translate mostly? Books?"

"Good heavens, no. Technical material mostly. For salesmen, engineers . . . anybody. Interpretation is slightly different. There, I am usually one of a team giving simultaneous translations at conferences, technical symposia and the like."

"How very interesting you must find it all."

"I like it. I am using my one skill."

"Good. Now, to return to your claim. I am sure the copy of the certificate you sent me is authentic, but you will appreciate that I must check it."

"You haven't already done so?"

"My dear sir, I only received it on Friday."

"As late as that? The posts in this country are getting worse."

"Delays are not infrequent. My fellow executor has, however, been informed of your intention to claim."

"And what did he say about that?"

"He was not best pleased. He wanted to know why you had not come forward before now. Incidentally, why have you waited so long since Mr Prior's death?"

"A few weeks only."

"True. But we have gone a long way towards settling the estate. Intervention now . . ."

"I only learned of my father's death about ten days ago."

"Then I really must congratulate you on the speed with which you got in touch with me. Incidentally, how did you learn that I was Mr Prior's solicitor?"

"Well, I . . ."

"Yes?"

"I . . . er . . . employed an enquiry agent. He had no difficulty."

"Still, he was very quick. You must let me have his name."

"Why?"

"Because I need to employ such people from time to time and I should be glad to know of somebody who would afford me such prompt service as you appear to have received. They charge by the day and they tend to take their time over even the most simple matters."

"I see. I will enquire at the bureau which I employed in Paris for the name of their British contact."

"Thank you. If you would let me have it . . . but where were we? Ah, yes! I must check on the certificate and then confer with my fellow executor. I think I can do that very quickly. It will only entail one journey to London. Then I can let you know definitely where we stand, Mr Gooding. So when shall I see you again? Would Wednesday afternoon be convenient?"

"Here? In Salisbury?"

"Why not, Mr Gooding? There is a great deal of money involved."

"But I am proposing to return to Paris."

"When?"

"As soon as possible."

"I see. In that case, as I am journeying to London, and you are staying there, perhaps we could meet at your hotel. The . . ." Pulker searched through his notes, ". . . the Vessan. That would save you another journey down here."

"Is there much point, Mr Pulker? You have already advised me that I cannot suppose you will recognise my claim and that I ought to get a solicitor to look after my interests."

"And I don't alter one word of it. It would be most improper of me to raise your hopes. But . . . and here I am speaking off the record, and what I am saying in no way constitutes a promise . . .

but my fellow executor is a prominent man, and the last thing he wants is to be involved in a legal wrangle in the courts, particularly a contest which would be certain to arouse a great deal of interest and, if you'll forgive me saying so, a great deal of undesirable publicity for his dead colleague who was, I may say, a highly respected man."

"He would want to avoid that?"

"At all reasonable cost."

"So that after checking my birth certificate and finding it genuine . . ."

"Quite, Mr Gooding. I should be obliged to give him the benefit of my advice, bearing in mind his own wishes. Were I to point out to him that your legal representative would have good cause to contest the will, he would almost certainly prefer to arrive at a legal accommodation with you. Because we would not be able to avoid the law entirely. Executors are not allowed to change the provisions of a will without the consent of the Probate Court. But if there were no contest, merely the presentation of an agreement, then the matter could be dealt with without causing comment. Do I make myself clear, Mr Gooding?"

Gooding nodded.

"Presumably you would like to know our attitude before your return to France?"

"Naturally."

"Excellent."

"May I know how much my father left?"

Pulker smiled. "I cannot divulge details of Mr Prior's estate to you. Not at the moment. But if, when we meet on Wednesday, I am in a position to suggest that we work towards an accommodation, then I shall be prepared to let you know the amounts involved. Indeed, I must do that, so that you know what you are about."

"I understand."

"Good. So although you are going away from here with no firm promises, I hope you will not assume that your journey has been entirely fruitless."

"I expected very little, Mr Pulker. I came merely to sound out the opposition, as it were."

"Not opposition, Mr Gooding, but—and here I am about to ask you a personal question which you are in no way obliged to answer—why on earth did you not make yourself known to Mr Prior during his lifetime? It would probably have meant that the situation we are now in could have been avoided."

Gooding frowned slightly. "I suppose I was guided by my mother. She and her husband brought me up well and gave me an adequate home, and she never mentioned my father. So he was, as far as I was concerned, a man who never existed. Then, later, when I had to get a job and go abroad to earn a living, there never seemed to be time to seek him out."

"A letter would have helped."

"Hardly a proper contact between a father and his son who had never met."

"Perhaps not. But if you didn't make the effort to meet him when he was alive, why make the effort now to profit from his estate? Do you think he owes you something?"

"He certainly owed my mother a great deal."

"I see."

"Can you see any reason why I should not benefit from my father's estate?"

"No. But neither can I see any valid reason for keeping him in ignorance of your existence. There would have been no complications. You would still have been a free agent, and at least you would have afforded him the pleasure of knowing he did not die childless. That thought was a great sorrow to him."

Gooding shrugged. "He never sought out my mother and me."

Pulker didn't reply. He got to his feet. "Until Wednesday morning, then, Mr Gooding. I shall call on you during the time I had intended to use in travelling back here, so shall we say ten o'clock?"

"That will be fine for me."

"That is settled then. I'll just get Fiona to show you out."

"Did you get him?" asked Reed.

Berger, sitting in the front passenger seat of the parked car and using the camera didn't reply until he had taken another shot of Gooding who had emerged from Pulker's office building and was now standing on the pavement looking about him.

"Three," grunted Berger. "Any more, do you think?"

"Just one, for luck. Aye, aye! He's not lost. He knows where he's going."

Gooding was striding away from them.

"That's the way to the station," said Berger, leaning over to put the camera on the back seat. "I'll take him."

As Berger got out of the car to follow their quarry on foot, Reed started the engine.

"I'll see you at the station, then."

"You're disappearing?"

"I can't drive slowly along behind you, can I?"

"You could stop round corners to see that he definitely is going for a train."

"I'll do what I can. Get going or you'll lose him."

"He's a right smarmy bastard, that one," said Green as he joined Wanda at the car.

"Did you get to know where his mother lives?"

"She's now Mrs Stringer and keeps a boarding house in Ryde."

"Isle of Wight. That means we want Lymington and the car ferry."

"No, love," replied Green. "Portsmouth and the ordinary boat. That goes straight into Ryde. We can park the car and cross on foot."

"You won't need the car in Ryde?"

"It's not that big and there's plenty of taxis."

Green strapped himself carefully into the front seat. It was an unaccustomed position for him. He much preferred the back, but the seat belt gave him confidence, and the opportunity to sit next to Wanda was a chance not to be missed for him.

As Wanda turned on to the A36 and headed for Southampton, she asked: "Does George know?"

"I phoned him. He sounded as though he'd had a bit of a tiring session with Kennard. But don't you worry about your old man, sweetie. He's a born comer-out-on-topper."

Wanda smiled. "He's very reliant on you, Bill."

"Is he now?" asked Green, unable to keep the pleasure out of his voice. "If you'd known us a few years ago you wouldn't have said that."

"I don't believe you. Oh, I've heard all about it. How you were always at daggers drawn, but George has told me that on looking back over the years he realises you've done him the greatest kindness of all."

"What's that?"

"You've never let him down." She smiled across at him. "He even told me about the time when he was feeling a bit prima donna-ish and had run out of his beloved tobacco and you made him smoke two of your cigarettes at once to make up for the loss of his pipe."

"Aye, well! We were in the same team. And as I always say, George is jammy."

"Only jammy?"

"All right. He's good, too. And, if you must have it, he's done me the odd good turn."

"Thank you, Bill. You see, George is everything to me, but you have a very special place, too. You're too inextricably mixed with him ever to be left out, and I would like my two favourite men to see as much good in each other as I do."

Not displeased, Green helped himself to a crumpled Kensitas and then proceeded to tell Wanda of the interview between Pulker and Gooding. When he had finished, Wanda asked: "You don't think he was telling the truth, do you?"

"I didn't see his face. That might have told me more."

"Did you tell George you thought he was a liar?"

"Yes."

"It's going to be difficult to prove. Then where are you?"

"Don't ask me, love."

They found a parking spot backing on to a building above the approach to the steamer. Green said: "I know these boats. Doris and I have used them for years. They can be draughty, even in summer."

"This suit is a warm one. There'll be some shelter, won't there? Behind something?"

"There's an indoors and at this time of year it won't be too packed."

They had to wait more than twenty minutes for the boat. As they stood within the queue corral, Green told Wanda he had decided that they would have lunch before finding Mrs Stringer. He knew a place, he said, where the fish and chips were wonderful.

They went aboard and, after the short crossing, took the train to Ryde station from the end of the pier. Green was wasting no time. Wanda got the impression that there was an urgency in her husband's assistant that she had never encountered before. They ate their meal with as much despatch as Green could decently manage and then, as they went down the hill to the station approach, he said: "We'll take a taxi to the local nick. It's not all that far, but a cab will be quicker."

"Can you give me the address of a boarding house kept by a Mr and Mrs Stringer?" asked Green after he had made himself known to the desk sergeant.

"They in trouble, sir?"

"Not so's you'd notice, but we've got our eye on her son in the smoke and I want to ask her a couple of questions."

"Nothing we should know about, then?"

"Not unless you can tell me who was the father of the illegitimate son she had in Leicester twenty-nine years ago."

"Like that, is it, sir. Now, the address."

"Do you know Mr and Mrs Stringer, Sergeant?" asked Wanda.

"No, ma'am. But they're all here in the hotel and boarding house list." He consulted the booklet. After a moment he asked: "You did say Stringer didn't you, sir?"

"That's right, lad."

"Well now, there's nobody of that name listed as keeping a boarding house. But wait a minute, there's the telephone directory."

Green lit a cigarette, but said nothing. Wanda took a seat opposite the desk.

"There's a few Stringers, sir, but which one . . ."

"How many, Sergeant?"

"One, two, three . . . eight, sir."

"Could you afford eight local calls?"

The sergeant shrugged and picked up the handset. As fruitless call succeeded fruitless call, Green remained silent. At last the desk sergeant put the phone down.

"That's it, Mr Green. No boarding house. Are you sure your info was good?"

"I'm sure I have what we were told, Sergeant. But it obviously wasn't good. So now I'll use the phone to call my chief if I may. Do I still have to dial trunks from here, or have you got STD now?"

"Stringer," said Green. "It was the first name that came into his head. He decided to string Pulker along."

"You're right, I'm afraid. By the same token he took us for a ride."

"What?"

"Ryde. You and Wanda."

Green grimaced. "What was his game?"

"I can only assume he wanted to fool Pulker or gain time for some reason. It was probably my fault. I instructed Pulker too carefully."

"He did it well."

"Too well?"

"You mean did he make it sound like a police interrogation? A bit perhaps, but he didn't even mention Prior's murder. He steered clear of mentioning any police activity."

Masters frowned. "Perhaps he should have talked about it. It would have been natural, wouldn't it?"

Kennard, in whose office the discussion was taking place, and who was present as Green made his report, said: "Solicitor talking to a murdered man's son for the first time like that? Yes, it would have been expected. Did Pulker even say he was sorry about Prior's death?"

Green shook his head.

"That would be strange, wouldn't it? You'd expect condolences from a lawyer."

"Maybe. I reckon it was a combination of things. Gooding got a bit upset when Pulker asked how he'd got to know who Prior's solicitor was. But that was after . . . wait a minute! Pulker made a thing of wanting to speak to his mother and it was after that . . .

yes, he hesitated a bit and then he gave her name, Stringer, although he hadn't been asked for it, and then he gave all that guff about her keeping a boarding house in Ryde."

Kennard said: "So he didn't want Pulker to approach her. Why?"

"Because she would blow the gaff."

"That's right. But . . ."

"Yes, lad?"

"At least we can assume she's still alive. If she'd been dead he'd have said fast enough."

Masters got to his feet.

"Bill, ring the Yard and ask them to check if there is such a place as the Vessan Hotel."

"The lads will be able to tell us that when they get through."

"Not if it doesn't exist. They'll be chasing Gooding who may be leading them anywhere."

"I get you." Green picked up the phone.

A few minutes later, with his hand over the mouthpiece, he said: "It exists. Do you want them to ask if Gooding is a guest?"

"I think not. We don't want to frighten him off."

"Fair enough." Green spoke a few more words into the phone and then put it down.

"I think he started to tell the truth," said Masters, "and then he panicked. Had he a reason for doing so?"

"What's going on?" demanded Kennard. "You're treating a perfectly simple claim to a will—whether it's good or bad—to the full Yard pressure. I want to know what's behind it."

"Your reputation, lad," retorted Green. He turned to Masters. "What next, George?"

"Reed and Berger," said Masters. "I want to hear from them."

"Give them a chance. It's barely six o'clock." Green opened up a new packet of Kensitas and for once was to be seen smoking a cigarette in pristine condition.

"I've written a bit of a timetable," said Kennard, pushing his writing pad across the table. "I've just jotted it down as you've been talking. Mr Green said Gooding reached Pulker's office at about a quarter to eleven, so that meant he caught the nine o'clock from Waterloo, and got in here, I think, at ten thirty-seven. That would give him eight minutes from the station, in a taxi, to get to Pulker."

"Good, lad. I like to see this sort of thing," said Green. "We don't do it very often. What's this? Gooding didn't leave Salisbury until twelve twenty-four?"

"He couldn't have done if his interview lasted half an hour as you said."

"More like twenty minutes."

"Ah! Well then he'd just have had time to catch the eleven twenty. But it would be by the skin of his teeth if he walked."

Masters said: "Assume it's the later one. What time did that reach London?"

"Two minutes past two."

"There you are then," said Green. "Four hours ago. The lads would have to see where he went and get any pictures they took developed . . ."

He was interrupted by the phone. Kennard lifted it and after listening for a moment, put it down.

"Sergeant Reed," he said. "In a hurry. He asked me to tell you he and Berger are trying to catch the six ten and will reach Salisbury at about ten to eight. They've got the car so they'll drive to Winterbourne Cardinal."

"Anything else?"

"He said he was in too much of a hurry to speak to you."

"Thank you."

"Don't get tetchy, George," warned Green. He turned to Kennard. "You've got to learn to live with His Nibs. He only gets like this when he's seen the light. Then he can't wait to put the lid on in case it jumps out and escapes."

"You mean he's on to something I don't know about?"

"Not only on to it lad, he's cracked it. Either that or he's feeling nervous because he's got to face his mother-in-law and report progress, and there's been very little of that today when it comes to hard fact that a civvy would appreciate."

"Cut it out," growled Masters. "I want to see the pathologist who did the post-mortem on Prior."

"What for?" asked Kennard suspiciously. "What's that got to do with Gooding trying to defraud the estate—if he is?"

"Please arrange for me to see him tomorrow morning."

"If he's free."

"Leave him in no doubt that I propose to see him."

It was twenty past eight when the sergeants arrived at Winter-bourne Cardinal.

"We waited dinner for you," said Masters. "So no report now. We'll give you ten minutes for a wash and a drink before we sit down."

"Poor loves," said Doris Green. "You do chase them about, George. They've been on the go since breakfast."

Masters nodded to the sergeants, who left the room, then he turned to Doris and said with a grin. "I'm only doing it to impress Bella. Discipline, devotion to duty . . ."

"George!" Bella said. "You are a humbug. I have never accused you of dereliction of duty."

"Nor I you of being a martyr to selective amnesia, but if you remember . . ."

"I remember quite well. I was guilty of . . ."

"Not you," said Green. "George is feeling the same as he always does when he reckons he's got it buttoned up. I'd like to bet that within an hour he makes some totally unexpected suggestion. Unexpected to us, that is, but not to him."

"In that case, what is it to be, George?" demanded Bella.

"At a guess? That we should all repair to The Grange public house immediately after dinner."

"And that will further your investigation?"

"It will be a nostalgic trip for William," said Wanda. "That's where, as a young man, he was . . ."

"Please, Wanda!" said Doris. "It's disgusting."

"Not it," said Green. "I shall love returning to my old haunts. I'll even point out the rail where I leaned over to . . ."

"Bill!"

The sergeants came in together at that point and Masters handed each of them a ready-prepared Scotch.

"Bring your drinks with you," suggested Bella, getting to her feet. "I'm sure William is drooling over the thought of jugged hare and it is cruel to make him wait any longer."

"Not 'arf," said Green. "Particularly after you told me it was being cooked in cider. "My old mum used to chop her onions so small that after she'd fried them with the mixed herbs . . ."

"Stop it," groaned Wanda. "This weekend is developing into a gastronomic nightmare for Doris. You'll tell us next that she has never given you jugged hare."

"Well . . . sometimes."

"Come on you old misery. Let's see what Ena Cully has made of it." She took his arm in hers and escorted him to the dining room.

As soon as they were sitting at the table and while Bella was still serving the joints of jugged hare in their highly aromatic gravy, Masters looked at Reed. "You're bursting to tell us all about it. So you might as well get it off your chest and then relax."

"It was really very easy, Chief. He walked from Mr Pulker's office to the station. Sergeant Berger tailed him and I drove. He'd just missed the eleven twenty, so he had to wait for the twelve twenty-four. As soon as he'd asked and been told he'd got an hour to wait, he went into a phone box and had twenty pence worth. Two tenpenny pieces."

"To the same number?"

"Yes, Chief. He didn't dial in between."

"Sorry. Go on."

"I expect he called London—spending that much."

"Yes."

"Then he had a second call. This time with two-pee pieces. Three of them."

"The caller lived fairly close by, then?"

"It would seem so, Chief, unless the cheap call was long distance, too. You can always pass a short message, such as the time a train will arrive, for a few pence."

"Of course. And we have no means of knowing, unless you got a good estimate of the length of each call."

"Sorry, Chief. I never thought to check."

"Try to remember, lad," said Green. "The four bob call? How long? If it was local, it would be a long, long call. If it was London, no time at all."

Berger said: "I think it was nearer than London. I think it was a long local job."

"And the cheaper one?"

"A few words long distance."

Green was gently easing a huge chunk of tender meat off a thick back joint. "It could be important," he said.

"Why?" asked Bella. "Why catechise that young man on the lengths of two phone calls?"

"Because . . ." and here Green turned the joint to perform the same operation on the other side of it, ". . . we reckon—that is, George and me—that there are two women that Gooding might get in touch with. One . . ." he paused while he completed his task, ". . . his mistress, in London. Two, his mother, we don't know where. Now, if he spent four bob on a long local call, it could be that he was giving his mother a full account of his meeting with Pulker, or warning her, or instructing her what to say. If that guess is right, it means his mother lives fairly near here and that is a help to us. But if the expensive call was to London, to his girl friend, it tells us nothing, because as Reed said a minute ago, you can pass a two word message to the other end of the country for a couple of pence. And if that's what happened, we're no further forward. But estimates of the lengths of the two calls would help us."

"I see. You do lead complicated lives, don't you?"

"They have their rewards. Take this jugged hare, now, and the jelly . . ."

"What next?" Masters asked Reed.

"He went into the station coffee shop. We did the same, one at a time. We got a few more mug shots, and then when the train came, we got on."

"Any difficulties?"

"None, Chief. He sat and read a paper. Berger and I travelled separately with him between us. Whichever way he went we would see him. He went to the loo just once."

"No suspicions."

"No, Chief. He got off at Waterloo, and there was this bit of capurtle waiting for him."

"Capurtle?" demanded Bella enquiringly.

"Frippet," said Green with his mouth full. "Girl, dame, bit of stuff, frail . . ."

"Thank you, William. Does the epithet capurtle carry with it any indication of the physical attributes of the girl in question?"

"And how! You'd have been a nifty bit of capurtle in your day. You've still got the figure for it, now, of course, but that blue rinse would eliminate you."

Wanda laughed. Masters choked and, oddly enough, Bella looked pleased. She had obviously liked the compliment to her figure.

"Go on, Reed," said Masters.

"There's not much else to tell you, sir. Gooding and his girl went to the Vessan Hotel."

"They did?" asked Green.

"Yes. We followed them in a taxi. No sweat."

"And?"

"They're registered as Mr and Mrs Gooding."

"That figures."

"That's it, Chief. Except for these." Reed drew an envelope from his pocket and handed it to Masters who tumbled the enclosed photographs onto the table. "Photographic did them as a special rush job for you, and Mr Boulderstone says you owe all his boys a drink for sending them to panic stations to get those prints."

Masters didn't reply. He examined two shots of Gooding and then handed them to Bella. "Does he favour Prior at all?"

Bella peered closely. "Not in the slightest. There is no resemblance. A completely different shape to the head."

"Thank you. What about his *petite amie*?" He handed over two head and shoulders shots of a dark-haired, small-boned woman who, by his estimate, would be in her early twenties.

Bella stared at them for a moment. "Are there any profiles?"

In silence Masters shuffled the prints. "Only one of the two of them together. Not a profile. More a back shot."

Green looked across at Masters, eyebrows raised. People's backs are usually reckoned by those who know to be as good a give-away as a face, particularly if there is movement.

Masters nodded almost imperceptibly. Bella gazed at the photograph and then again at all three. "You said you had never accused me of being a martyr to selective amnesia, George. Now you really can accuse me of genuine, albeit intermittent, forgetfulness. In other words, these pictures ring a bell. But which one I cannot remember. Is she a model whose photograph I have seen in a paper?" She frowned with renewed concentration. "She doesn't appear in a television commercial, does she? One of those that rely on French accents to be different?"

"Don't try to force it," said Masters. "Let's finish dinner." He included both Reed and Berger in his next remark. "Thank you. You both did remarkably well."

Berger shrugged. "How, Chief? A few mug shots . . ."

"Wait and see, lad," counselled Green. "Eat up. We're going out afterwards."

CHAPTER VII

WANDA AND DORIS Green announced that they intended to accompany their husbands to The Grange. Wanda because she had seen very little of her husband all day and Doris because her husband insisted on his wife visiting the spot where, as he put it, the landlord had done him during the war. The two sergeants were very pleased to accept Masters' suggestion that they should stay behind and keep their hostess company. The day had already been long enough for them.

The quartet walked the short distance to the pub. Wanda, with her arm in that of her husband, asked: "It was unlike mummy not to be able to recognise a face if she knew it. Do you think she had seen it before?"

"Almost certainly."

"Did the fact that she said it rang a bell help you at all?"

Doris Green interrupted. "These two looked very self-satisfied when Bella was looking at the snap. I noticed them exchanging glances. Were you laughing at her, Bill?"

"Get out of it," said Green. "We were tickled pink by what she said."

"But she said nothing," protested Wanda.

"She did, love she did."

"Did she really?" Wanda asked Masters.

"Heaps," affirmed her husband.

"Tell us," pleaded Doris. "You men are always so secretive."

Masters took Doris Green with his free arm.

"Bella had obviously seen that girl at some time. That was very obvious. But she couldn't recall where or when because she was casting her mind back in the wrong direction. Mrs Gooding—we might as well call her that as she is masquerading as his wife—

153

looked a bit like a fashion plate in those photographs. As she would. A young Parisienne visiting London would wear her best bib and tucker, wouldn't she? And she's a personable looking girl. That caused Bella to think of models, ad-girls and starlets. A natural mistake. But what she ought to have done was to come much nearer home and to see our little friend in a very different setting and a very different role."

"I'm still lost," said Wanda.

"How about here, in the village of Winterbourne Cardinal?"

"You really mean that? Doing what?"

"Working as a barmaid or waitress at The Grange."

The two women stopped as one.

"You're joking," said Doris.

"I'm not," replied Masters, urging them forward. "Ask Bill."

"True enough. Why do you think we're on our way to the pub now?"

"But George said we'd be going there long before he even saw those photographs."

"He said he guessed we would be going. The photos only confirmed it. Look, love, your old man expected this, but he had to have the mugshots to show to the landlord before he could make enquiries about Gooding's mistress."

"I see. Shall we get a drink, or will Doris and I just have to stand around while you two make your enquiries?"

"Naughty! Come on, up the steps, and don't forget to wipe your nose on the boot scraper."

"Bill!"

The landlord, Alec Pugsley, had met Masters on a previous occasion and remembered him.

"Good evening, Mr Masters. I heard you were down here. And Mrs Masters, too. Glad you could drop in to see us."

"Nice to be here, Alec. Could I have four brandies, with ginger ale?"

"Of course. Your party has found a table. Shall I bring them over?"

"If you please."

"Ice and lemon?"

"Lemon. No ice."

"Oh, I do like this, Bill," said Doris, easing her shoulders out of her coat and draping it on the back of the chair. "It's really nice."

"That's because you're in the cocktail bar, not in the spit-and-sawdust like me and my mates last time I was here. And it's not the same landlord. The one who was here then would be a hundred and five by now."

The landlord came across with the tray of drinks. As Masters paid, he asked Pugsley: "You don't seem to be terribly busy in here, Alec, so could I have a few minutes of your time?"

Pugsley's immediate reaction was to agree, but then it seemed as if he suddenly recalled that Masters was a senior policeman. His ready response faded from his lips and a certain degree of caution crept into his tone. Instead of saying yes, he asked what for?

"Not got a guilty conscience have you, chum?" asked Green.

"Not that I know of, but it always feels as if I had when a policeman starts to ask questions. It's the business, you see. So many rules and regulations you can break—serving under age, after time, when a customer's already had too much and so on."

"I don't think we shall be involving you personally in anything of that nature, Alec. All I want to ask you is if you've ever seen this girl before." Masters handed him a photograph from the packet.

Despite the subdued lighting, Pugsley had no hesitation in saying: "That's Robbie."

"You know her?"

"I should do. A little French piece. She worked in the dining room here for a few weeks at the end of the summer."

"You said her name was Robbie."

"That's right. Robbie Vignal. What's she done? It can't be work permits, because she's in the EEC, being French, and I wouldn't have taken her on unless I'd been satisfied it was legal to employ her."

"I'm not suggesting you've done anything illegal, Alec. My interest is in the girl only. She's turned up in London and . . ."

"Here, wait a minute, Mr Masters. When did she turn up in London?"

"She's there now. Why do you ask?"

"Because she left here in a bit of a hurry, saying she'd got to get back to France to a new job. From what she told me she wasn't expecting to come back to England again."

Masters smiled. "Well, now, Alec, she is back and keeping company with a chap we've got our eye on. So you see why we're asking."

"Yes, yes I do. But you'll have to excuse me, ladies and gentlemen. I've got customers waiting at the bar."

"Please come back as soon as you've served them."

"You've struck oil, George," said Green. "Robbie Vignal. Sounds more like a boy's name to me."

"Nonsense, Bill," said his wife. "We call girls Jo these days—short for Josephine. Robbie—that's probably short for Roberta, whatever that is in French."

"Robert is the same in both countries," said Wanda. "Probably her name is the feminine of that—Robertte—with another *t* and an *e* on the end."

Masters didn't join in. He waited silently until Pugsley returned.

"Now, Mr Masters, that's everybody fixed up for another few minutes. So you'd better tell me what young Robbie's got herself into."

"As yet, nothing, Alec. But as I say, we have to make enquiries about her because she has arrived over here with a man we suspect of attempted fraud. She may be innocent of anything . . . so tell me how you came to employ her at The Grange."

"Well, now," said Pugsley, "that's a funny thing. Mrs Hapgood —you wouldn't know her, but she was housekeeper to the late Mr Prior. You'd know about him, of course."

"I'd heard he'd been shot in the woods."

"That's right. And those dam'fool policemen—begging your pardon, Mr Masters—have arrested Sid Lunn for it and charged him with murder. Sid Lunn wouldn't hurt a human being . . ."

"I'd heard that people think the police have made a mistake."

"Of course you would have, staying with Mrs Bartholomew, and her going to marry Mr Prior."

"Mrs Hapgood?"

"Oh, yes. Well it appears young Robbie had come over to England and like a lot of these youngsters, had run out of money before she wanted to go back. She found herself in these parts without tuppence ha'penny to call her own. One morning she knocked on the door at Brooksbank—that was Mr Prior's house—and when Mrs Hapgood answered, said she'd been told in the village that they wanted a girl to do housemaid or general duties. She'd gone to apply for the job."

"It isn't often you get girls applying for a job as a housemaid these days," said Wanda. "I suppose Mrs Hapgood was surprised."

"So she was, Mrs Masters. But she didn't need any help up there, having only Mr Prior to look after. So she began to tell Robbie that whoever had sent her to Brooksbank had made a mistake, when Mr Prior happened along. When he heard the problem, he told Robbie I needed a waitress in my dining room."

"How would he know that?" asked Green.

"Because he came here every lunch time. He had lunch here. Like Mrs Masters said, waitresses aren't all that easy to find. Not good ones. And they're always wanting to go off on holiday in the summer, and that's our busiest time. It was no secret that I was in the market for a girl to help in the dining room."

"So she came to you and you gave her a job?"

"Why not? She was a nice looking girl, French, with an accent people liked to hear, and she was pretty good waiting on. I wouldn't have minded if she'd stayed."

"Thank you," said Masters. "When did she leave?"

"Let me see, now . . . it would be about . . . yes, about the time Mr Prior died, or just a few days after."

"To go back to France?"

"Yes."

"Where did she live while she was here?"

"With Mrs Dolman. That's the cottage practically next door. She hadn't anywhere to stay, so my missus got her fixed up there."

"I see. Thank you again, Alec. That's all I wanted to know. I'm sure she was a great asset in your dining room."

"She was that."

"And I suppose Mr Prior got extra special treatment from her because he'd virtually found her the job?"

"That's right. She was grateful to him. Made a point of always serving him herself and giving him a bit of advice on what was best on the menu and seeing he had the best bit of cheese and so on."

"A nice girl, in fact."

"That's right, Mr Masters. That's why I can't see her running about with somebody you're interested in."

"These young lasses!" sighed Green. "There's no telling who they'll get mixed up with these days."

"I suppose you're right. Now, sir, if you'll excuse me . . ."

"Another round here please, Alec, when you've got time."

Kennard had phoned during their absence to say that the pathologist would see them at ten thirty the next morning in his office at the hospital. Reed also had a report to make.

"We didn't mention it at dinner, Chief, but while we were in the office we arranged to be told if Gooding or Vignal tried to leave the country."

"You didn't ask for a watch to be kept."

"It didn't seem warranted, Chief. But we did say that if anybody was passing the Vessan . . ."

"Nothing to alarm them, I hope?"

"No, Chief. I stressed that. I got a call just after you went out. They've gone off to a club for the evening, so it looks as if they're staying put."

"I'm glad to hear it."

"You seem," said Bella, "to be concentrating on the fraudulent claim more than the charge of murder against Lunn. No doubt you have your reasons."

Masters replied: "The two cases are connected, Bella. And just to whet your appetite, may I ask you if you ever had a meal with Haydn Prior at the local pub?"

"Never. He lunched there. But I never did."

"Then you must have seen the girl in the photograph in the village at some time."

"The model? Oh, no . . . wait! Wait a minute! She was

French. That's right. I saw her talking to Haydn once. He told me who she was. But she was in jeans and a blouse then and her hair . . . yes, her hair was tied up in a blue scarf." She regarded Masters severely. "Are you trying to tell me that Haydn was having an affaire with that girl?"

"The thought had never occurred to me until now. I swear it."

"It's just as well, otherwise I would have known you were barking up the wrong tree."

Dr Orr, the pathologist, was an autocratic-looking man. He was middle-aged, and wore a blue, chalk-stripe suit with waistcoat and watch chain. His face was deeply lined, giving an appearance of heavy jowls whereas he was, in reality, not fleshy. He wore rimless glasses which gleamed as brightly as his highly polished black shoes. The creases in his trousers were perfect, his shirt gleaming white, and his semi-stiff white collar held the club tie well out from his chest. His hair, now greying, was close-trimmed and pomaded. The whole appearance of the man was—whilst instilling confidence in his patients—calculated to impress upon them that here was a man who knew what was best for them and would brook no argument, not even a question, concerning their health and his care of it.

He adopted this attitude with Masters—at first. Kennard, who had accompanied him and Green, made the introductions.

"I can see no reason for this discussion, Superintendent. To determine the cause of death was a simple matter. Undisputably a massive heart attack. Consequent upon over-exertion following gunshot wounds."

Masters, sitting opposite to the consultant, inclined his head in agreement. "We do not question your finding, Doctor. We are seeking to establish the cause of the cause."

"The cause was the heart attack. The cause of the cause, undue exertion, and the cause of the cause of the cause a gunshot wound." It was said in a tone which indicated that the interview was over before it had fairly begun.

"You found parachlorophenylalanine in the body in large amounts."

"I also found potatoes and other food."

"You would expect the latter, but not the former."

"Mr Masters, the finding of a non-toxic drug is to be expected as often as not on these occasions. I have already been pestered by a young solicitor, Sibbald, concerning the presence of this substance, and I will give you the answer I gave him. PCPA is not lethal, nor did it contribute either directly or indirectly to Prior's death. That is my opinion and I shall testify to that effect in court."

"Directly I can accept. Indirectly I cannot accept."

"You are questioning my professional expertise, Mr Masters?"

"Seeking, rather, to build upon it to widen the scope of my own knowledge and, consequently, my ability to investigate the circumstances in which Mr Prior met his death."

"I see." The tone was slightly supercilious. "Tell me, Superintendent, what you know about PCPA—a drug, I should warn you, that very few medical men know anything of."

"And I am no medical man. But I understand that PCPA inhibits the synthesis of serotonin in the brain and this leads to total insomnia."

"You're wrong."

"Really? I thought that Jouvet, the French trialist, showed that the two great systems of sleep—hindbrain and forebrain—are triggered and sustained by different neuro- and bio-chemical mechanisms. And that both human and animal studies in this context have shown the importance of serotonin."

"You appear to have done your homework, Mr Masters. But while agreeing on the importance of serotonin, I cannot agree that PCPA inhibits its synthesis."

"And yet several experts have investigated this very point and have come to the opposite conclusion."

"I am aware of that. But were you to read more widely you would find this fact disputed."

"Would you please tell me, doctor, if it does not inhibit the synthesis of serotonin, exactly what PCPA does do?"

"PCPA has a great many actions. It is not a drug which many doctors would care to use widely."

"You are saying that it is an unpredictable drug? That you

could not foresee what reaction a patient would have to it?"

"That is precisely why I have said no responsible doctor would use it widely."

"That suggests that you cannot list all the effects it might have."

"Just so."

"Yet you can state categorically that it will not inhibit the synthesis of serotonin?"

"Yes."

"Even though some eminent men in this field have investigated this very point and have come to the opposite conclusion?"

"British investigators have never been able to reproduce the findings of the French investigators, even though they have deliberately set out to do so."

"That leaves the French investigators looking rather silly, doesn't it?"

Orr looked down his nose, but made no reply.

"Does chauvinism enter into this, Doctor? Would you, for instance, have a pecking order among trialists? British first, American second, German third, Japanese fourth and so on?"

"I certainly tend to trust some countries before others, simply because I believe them to have more reliable medical criteria."

"I can understand that. We all place more reliance in some people than others. But please tell me if you know of any drug which performs either predictably or safely in one hundred per cent of humans?"

"There is no such drug. Some have high strike rates, of course. The majority are, however, efficacious in—at a guess—seventy per cent of cases, maybe eighty per cent."

"Would that be true with a very famous drug like penicillin?"

"Of course. It is by no means effective in all cases for which it is prescribed and, of course, it can be dangerous if given to those who are allergic to it."

"Quite. How successful would penicillin have been if, after its successful initial trial, it had been tested on another group of people who, by chance, were all members of the group in which it is either non-effective or dangerous?"

"That would be highly improbable. Its strike rate is too high."

"But can you not have a drug where the strike rate is low? A drug which will have a certain effect in a few, and not in a majority?"

Orr considered this for a moment or two. Then—

"I see the logic of your argument. In theory, the answer is yes. In practice, no, because no manufacturer would market a drug which had a low strike rate, simply because it would not be an economical proposition. Doctors require a high degree of reliability, for obvious reasons. Do not, however, confuse a drug with a low strike rate with one that is rarely used. There are many of the latter. All excellent, life-saving products, which, in spite of not being commercial successes, are nevertheless made—at a loss, very often—to cater for the few cases in which they are needed."

"In theory, I am right, you said. Is it not, therefore, possible that PCPA, a drug which, in your own words, has a great many actions, some of which are unpredictable, has certain effects in a minority of humans?"

"I suppose it is."

"Then I must ask you if it is not possible that the French investigators discovered that in a minority of humans, PCPA caused total insomnia?"

For the first time, Orr removed the mask of autocracy. "You could just be right," he conceded, and then added drily, "after all, they were very small trials."

Masters sat back.

"I believe Prior was one of that minority."

Orr also sat back in his desk chair and gazed at him. "And that is what you will suggest in court."

"No, sir. You must do it, should the occasion arise."

"But I did not do a brain study. I have no proof of serotonin levels."

"Maybe not. But in the last week of his life, Prior, who was normally a sound sleeper, became, inexplicably, a total nonsomniac. That we can prove. He also consulted his GP because of it. That can be proved. You found the PCPA in the body. In vast amounts. All circumstantial evidence to prove that Prior was under the influence of the drug."

162

"Very well. But what is the point? He still died of a heart attack."

"So he did. But have you asked yourself why a sober-living man should be out of his bed and in a spinney in the small hours of a cold morning?"

Orr sat up. "Good heavens! Are you saying that he had reached the stage where a psychotic syndrome developed?"

"It was the fifth night without sleep."

"The fifth, eh? Hang on a moment."

Orr rose and went to his bookcase. After selecting a book he spent a moment or two seeking the section he wanted. He returned to his seat. "Here we are. Sleep deprivation. Fifth night. We're right. Psychotic syndrome by then. Gross disturbances of reality which may persist for varying periods; hallucinatory experiences become more prolonged and vivid; intermittent clouding of consciousness; disorientation in time, place and person; paranoia. And this is interesting. By night the picture resembles a delirious state." He closed the book and looked up. "It wouldn't be hard to guess how or why he was in the wood."

"Thank you, Doctor. Now, just one more point. The defendant, Lunn, claims that he was unaware of Prior's presence until Prior leapt out on him. This frightened Lunn temporarily, and his automatic reaction was to fire. He says he mistook the initial rustling, before Prior leapt out, to be the noise made by some animal, so he already had his finger on the trigger and the gun pointed."

Orr spread his hands. "I can guess what you're going to ask me. In his state, Prior could well have been most frightening. Capering, posturing, screeching. All very frightening at any time. On a dark night in a wood . . . I doubt very much whether Lunn could have helped firing if he was in the firing position. He would tense with fear and surprise. His muscles would contract, including that of the finger on the trigger. I imagine a poacher's gun is hair-triggered, isn't it? A very small squeeze could well have operated it."

"Thank you, Doctor." Masters got to his feet. "You have been most helpful."

Orr also rose. "It sounds as if we could have been instrumental in squashing the case against Lunn."

"That may well be so. But you could also have helped us to pin the crime squarely where it belongs. On the people who administered the PCPA."

"Quite. You know who that is?"

"We think so."

At last Orr smiled. "The cause behind the cause of the cause of the cause?"

"That's it, Doctor. Linked with a criminal conspiracy to defraud. Thank you for your time."

"It has been a pleasure to see how carefully you work, Mr Masters."

"Well, lad," said Green to Kennard as they left the hospital, "could you have put up a performance like His Nibs here?"

"Don't be so daft. I didn't know what they were talking about half the time. All I managed to get hold of was that I haven't got a case against Sid Lunn."

"I really don't think you have," agreed Masters. "But you will have a case, of that I'm sure."

"Who against? Somebody fed poor old Prior with this stuff . . ."

"PCPA?"

"That's right. But who?"

"Oh, come on, lad," said Green as they got into the car. Kennard shrugged. "It can't be Gooding. He was in France at the time."

"But his girl friend wasn't. Look, chum, it is fairly obvious that while Gooding stayed in France, he had to have somebody here in Winterbourne Cardinal to do his dirty work. He sent Robbie Vignal. But I was forgetting, you don't know very much about it yet, do you?"

"If you ask me, I know nothing about anything in this case."

"I'll let you have the full story," promised Masters, "but first things first. We've got to arrest Gooding and Vignal. Mr Kennard, how soon can you get a warrant? Conspiracy should cover it, but if whoever signs the ticket wants more, tell him we'll be adding attempted fraud and g.b.h."

"G.b.h.? You can't mean that. They didn't touch him."

"You can cause grievous bodily harm by feeding drugs just

as easily as you can with a cosh or a boot."

"Oh!"

"How soon?"

"Straight away. One or two JPs live close-by in Amesbury."

"Fine. Would you like Reed and Berger to collect our suspects? They've got to be brought here, of course, but my sergeants are more accustomed than you are to operating in London."

"That'll suit me," said Kennard. "I'd better have the names of the two we're after."

After supplying the necessary information, Masters looked at his watch. "It's barely eleven thirty. If the sergeants go by road, they'll be back by teatime."

"And the rest."

"It's only eighty-four miles from Salisbury, and most of the way is on good roads."

"They'll do it," said Green confidently.

At Masters' request, Colegrave called a meeting in his office at eight o'clock that evening. Besides the Chief Superintendent, the four members of the Yard team were present, together with Kennard and, at Masters' request, the two solicitors, Pulker and Sibbald.

The preliminaries over, Colegrave asked Masters to speak.

"The first I knew of Prior's death was when I was informed by Mrs Bartholomew on Friday evening that she had consented to marry him. That being so, she was naturally upset by his murder and anxious that the crime should be brought home to those responsible. But her bitterness was not general. She was convinced that Lunn, whom everybody in the area knew and liked, could not have been the culprit, even though he had fired the shot which wounded her fiancé.

"Almost immediately after I had heard this, Mr Pulker informed Mrs Bartholomew that he had just heard from a Harry Gooding, who claimed to be Prior's illegitimate son, and, therefore, a man in a position to claim a substantial portion of Prior's not inconsiderable fortune. The claim was supported by a photostat copy of an apparently genuine birth certificate.

"Not unnaturally, as they were to become man and wife, Prior and Mrs Bartholomew had spoken of intimate matters. One of these was Prior's sorrow at having no children. He confided that this had been due to no lack of desire for children on the part of his wife or, indeed, her physical inability to do so. The inability was his. He was infertile, proven so during his time in Cambridge by some of the leading authorities in this field.

"Gooding's claim, therefore, was immediately suspect. Mr Green and I, being in a position to do so, started discreet enquiries, and established that the nurse who assisted the doctor who carried out the tests on Prior had been named Gooding. Furthermore, we learned that she had left Cambridge soon after. It was an open secret that she was, though unmarried, expecting a baby. Our conclusion was that, after giving birth to the child she had been obliged to register it. When asked to name the father, she gave—for reasons of her own—the most respectable name she could think of without impugning the name of any doctor with whom she had worked. I should add at this point that we have traced the former Nurse Gooding. Her son has now co-operated by giving us her name and address. Mr Green has interviewed her and his report states that our supposition was correct. She was a flighty girl and spread her favours rather wide. As a result, she did not know who the real father was, so she chose Prior, because, as she said, she felt sorry for him. She also confirmed that Prior had never been involved with her in any way except as a patient. I should also tell you that Mr Green reports that she is now, and has been for many years, a highly respectable and happily married matron who is greatly distressed by her son's actions and has co-operated with us to the full."

"Nice woman," said Green. "Regrets what she did."

Kennard snorted. "A fine time to be sorry!"

Masters paused a moment to see if there were any further remarks before continuing.

"Mr Pulker told us Gooding was resident in Paris and intended to call at his office yesterday morning. It seemed strange to us that a death in an English village, which had not been reported widely, but merely inserted in the obituary column of the *Daily Telegraph*, should have become known to a man in Paris.

Further, we wondered how that same man could have known that Mr Pulker was Prior's solicitor.

"Mr Pulker informed us that Prior's estate was quite large and, therefore, to the criminal mind, definitely worth making a play for. On Saturday afternoon, Mr Pulker very kindly showed us over Brooksbank, Mr Prior's home. While we were there we learned that Mr Prior had been a keen radio ham. Furthermore, his log book told us that he had been in touch with another ham to whom he announced various snippets of private information such as the fact that he and Mrs Bartholomew were shortly to be married.

"We asked Sergeants Reed and Berger, who were in London at the time, to trace the owner of the call sign to which Prior had made these rather private revelations. It turned out that the licence belonged to an Englishman named Gooding."

"No wonder you started putting two and two together," said Colegrave. "But if you hadn't seen that log book it would have been a different matter."

"It would have taken us longer," admitted Green. "That is, if we had been called in officially."

"Quite right," resumed Masters. "The French wanted to know why we were interested. Reed and Berger didn't know, while Mr Green and I weren't there to supply the answer. The French, suspicious as hell, thought we were stalling, so they approached the Assistant Commissioner. He wanted to know what the DCI and I were up to. When I told him he instructed me to make my number with the local police just in case the case blew up and it appeared that we were working behind the backs of the people whose territory we were on."

Masters addressed Colegrave. "So we came to you, sir, and Mr Kennard, on Sunday afternoon and told you what we were up to. As a result of this, you very kindly invited us to help sort the whole business out. I suspect that even then you foresaw that the death and the false claim could be linked."

"Don't credit me with too much foresight. I had a gut feeling that the case against Sid Lunn was just too easy."

"I see. On Sunday afternoon Mr Kennard allowed me to see the Lunn file. The post-mortem report from the pathologist showed the presence of parachlorophenylalanine—known as PCPA for short. I decided to check up on that. The amount shown by Dr Orr turned out to be much bigger than a doctor would prescribe, and reference to medical papers showed that PCPA is a rather unpredictable drug. It can, and in some cases does, produce total insomnia, with hallucinations and derangement. I was interested, because Mrs Bartholomew had told me that Prior behaved very strangely in the week before his death.

"But Prior's GP had not prescribed PCPA for his insomnia. Only the usual sleeping pills. So where did the PCPA come from? Nearly all the work on the drug was French. In other words, it was likely to be more readily available in Paris than in Winterbourne Cardinal. France again, you see.

"I learned that, apart from the breakfast he had at home, Prior had very little food that didn't come from The Grange where he lunched each day, or Mrs Bartholomew's house where he usually had supper. I was also told that at lunchtime he was an inveterate taker of soup. I must confess that I had little hesitation in precluding Mrs Bartholomew's house. But soup was an ideal vehicle for the giving of daily doses of PCPA, and the soup was taken at The Grange.

"I said earlier that we wondered how Gooding could have got to know of Prior's death and the fact that Mr Pulker was his solicitor. It argued local—knowledge. So, local knowledge and PCPA in the soup at the local! An accomplice, without a doubt. For obvious reasons we suspected a woman, and Gooding was living with a woman—a Mlle Robbie Vignal—whom he had brought across to London with him.

"We got photographs of her. They were instantly recognised by the landlord at The Grange. Robbie had worked for him for several weeks as a waitress. During that time she had regularly waited upon Prior, and had left with no warning very soon after his death."

"Wait, wait!" said Colegrave. "How had she managed to engineer the exact job she needed if she was to poison Prior?"

"Very easily, sir. They knew Prior's address and Gooding must have known that help in a house is not easy to come by in England. So he sent Robbie to Brooksbank to offer her services as maid of all work. She would have been in the ideal position to do her stuff had she got in there, which she confidently expected to do. But Mrs Hapgood, Prior's housekeeper didn't need her. However, Prior knew that Pugsley at The Grange was always chronically in need of domestic staff. So Prior sent Robbie there, no doubt telling her that he patronised the restaurant himself regularly."

"So he actually engineered his own death in a way?"

"I'm afraid so."

"I'm a bit worried," said Kennard. "This PCPA stuff wouldn't kill him, so what was the point of going to all that trouble to feed it to him?"

"A good question. Gooding was told by Prior, over the radio, that he, Prior, was about to marry again. This didn't please Gooding. He had already decided to lay claim to the estate of the man named on his birth certificate as his father. He felt that he could succeed were Prior to die a widower. But if Prior were to remarry, the widow would have prior and inalienable claim on the estate at her husband's death."

"Did Gooding know Prior was not his father?"

"Mrs Stringer says she told him. And I think his subsequent actions show he was aware of it. If he had genuinely believed Prior to be his father, he would have made himself known. But he couldn't do this, because Prior could refute the claim, not only by disclaimer, but by the results of medical tests. So Gooding could make no approach during Prior's lifetime. This he accepted just so long as Prior remained a widower. But when Prior's intended marriage was announced, he could see the prize slipping away from him. So he had to think again.

"Mr Pulker will tell you that he questioned Gooding about his job. It appears that he is a language graduate with an ability to pick up a working knowledge of almost any tongue. With his expertise he found employment in what has become a mushroom industry since the formation of the Common Market—translation and interpretation. You will appreciate that, as often as not, the papers he had to translate were technical. Many of them sales literature and instruction books. Occasionally they were medical."

"Ah!" said Colegrave. "He got ideas from what he read."

"Not only ideas, sir, but contacts, too. Robbie Vignal was

secretary to a French hospital doctor whose trial reports Gooding translated. He met her while this was going on, and they started to live with each other shortly afterwards."

"How do you know all this?" asked Sibbald.

"I have had an opportunity to question them. Mr Green and I were able to show them that we knew so much about them before they were arrested, that they co-operated fully in order to prove to us that they meant no lasting harm to Prior."

"They didn't actually kill him," reminded Pulker.

"True. Nor apparently did they intend to, if we are to believe them. But to return to the narrative. Prior told Gooding over the air that he was about to remarry. Gooding wanted to stop the marriage. The only question was how to achieve this. As I told you earlier, much of the work on PCPA was done in France. Robbie's boss was one of the trialists, and it was reports of his trials that Gooding had translated. So he knew that PCPA caused total insomnia and that this led to disorientation and hallucination and so on. In layman's terms, it drove the recipient mad. The little plot he cooked up was to feed Prior PCPA to send him crackers. He thought it unlikely that the woman to whom Prior was engaged would consent to marry a man who was demonstrably *non compos mentis*."

"He'd likely be in a loony-bin in any case," said Kennard.

"The neatness of the plot from Gooding's point of view was the fact that Robbie could get hold of the PCPA. Don't forget, we're talking about very small amounts. Four grams a day is a huge dose, and that is about an eighth of an ounce. So a few ounces would go a very long way.

"So Gooding had the means and he had the motive. All he needed was the opportunity. He and Robbie manufactured it between them. It should be easy to get a job in Prior's household in view of the chronic shortage of domestic help in Britain."

"Risky, though," said Kennard. "On the spot. Bound to be suspected."

"Of what, lad?" asked Green. "If a housemaid's employer goes bonkers, what is there to suspect? Nothing. And certainly you don't go round looking for who drove him crackers, do you?"

"I get the point."

"Fairly foolproof," conceded Colegrave.

"But Gooding and Vignal had reckoned without the estimable Mrs Hapgood, the housekeeper at Brooksbank. She didn't want help in the house, because she herself was shortly leaving and Prior would be well served by Mrs Bartholomew and her equally estimable Ena Cully.

"However, Robbie had a stroke of luck. She and Gooding were correct in believing that there is always need for domestic help. The help required in Winterbourne Cardinal was by Alec Pugsley, landlord of The Grange. He wanted a waitress. Prior knew this because he lunched at the pub every day. And it was he who, having overheard her ask Mrs Hapgood for a job, sent her to Alec Pugsley. So she was in a position to serve Prior each day and to doctor his food. He was a consistent soup taker and so to put a pinch of PCPA in the plate was an easy matter, though I suspect to scatter it on any food would have been easy enough.

"The plan succeeded. Prior quickly became a nonsomniac and began to suffer the consequences of total deprivation. I won't go into the details now, but Prior behaved very strangely and unpredictably. He rang people up in the small hours, had periods of forgetfulness and so on. It would not have been long before his state would have become desperate and, I suppose, would have achieved its objective of putting off the marriage."

"Permanently?" asked Colegrave. "I mean, if he'd been taken into some hospital or institution, wouldn't he have recovered in time?"

"Undoubtedly."

"So the scheme would have failed."

"I think not. It could have been repeated fairly easily as soon as he was discharged. Then what? How often can a man be taken away, mentally deranged, before he becomes so tainted as to make any woman wary of marrying him or—and this I suspect would be the most likely result—before he, himself, dismissed the idea of ever remarrying?"

Colegrave nodded. "Then what would have happened?"

Masters grimaced. "I shall have to speculate. But I reckon Gooding is a clever rogue. It is my belief that he intended to establish himself as Prior's son."

"How on earth could he have done that?" asked Pulker.

"Quite easily, I believe. Prior is taken into a home as mentally deranged and a well set-up young man arrives to visit him. He announces himself to the staff as Prior's son. If Prior disclaims him, it is taken as a facet of his psychosis. Particularly if, next day, Gooding arrives again with his birth certificate, which is a genuine document, even if it is erroneous in naming Prior as the father. Gooding pitches a yarn to get sympathy. He is the illegitimate son and Prior has always fought shy of recognising him. But Prior is his father and so he considers it his duty to visit the old man in times of trouble in spite of non-recognition. And so on."

"Clever. He'd get sympathy all right."

"Quite. And how many times would it have to happen before Gooding became recognised? He would soon build up a fund of goodwill as the son who, despite being disowned by his father, came to visit him et cetera, et cetera. Powerful background evidence, eh Mr Pulker?"

"As you say, Superintendent. With Mrs Bartholomew no longer concerned, who would know that Prior had been proved infertile? Those who carried out the tests may never have got to hear of Gooding, or may even have been dead by the time Prior died."

"So where are we?" asked Kennard.

"You were present this morning when Dr Orr gave it as his opinion that with Prior acting under the influence of PCPA, Lunn cannot be blamed for firing inadvertently. So my advice is to ask the magistrates to free Lunn on a minute bail, explaining that when his case comes up, the Crown will proffer no evidence."

"I second that," said Sibbald.

"Gooding and Vignal are in your cells. I leave them to you, Mr Colegrave."

"Thanks."

"Young Kennard here wanted a meaty case," said Green. "Let him get his teeth into this one. He'll enjoy it."

The meeting broke up shortly afterwards. Everybody had left the office except Colegrave and Masters.

"I'm grateful to you for letting us in on this without too much inter-force umbrage being taken, sir. I was, I'll admit, surprised that you made your decision so readily on Sunday afternoon."

Colegrave grinned. "Don't be. You see, George, Dr Orr had rung me earlier. He told me young Sibbald had phoned him to ask a lot of questions about PCPA."

"Yes, sir?"

"I know young Sibbald. He's a nice chap, but he isn't bright enough to think up for himself the questions he'd asked Orr. I reckoned somebody had been coaching him."

"Ah! I wonder who that could have been?"

"I wondered the same thing. But when I heard you were in the area . . . don't worry, I didn't tell Kennard."

"Thank you, sir."

Masters had let Green tell it the second time. They were all there in the sitting room. Bella, Wanda and Doris, Reed and Berger. Masters acted as unobtrusive barman and kept the glasses filled as Green—his memory as good as ever—told their tale.

He had just finished, and the three women were singing their praises when Ena Cully entered, scowling.

"Now that that's over," she announced, "you can come through here for supper. It's nearly midnight, and if you think I'm keeping it hot any longer, you're mistaken."

"Heavens above," said Bella. "I'd forgotten you men hadn't eaten."

"What's for grub?" Green asked Ena Cully.

"Beef in beer."

"Beef in beer? That sounds good enough for me to excuse you."

"Excuse me? What for?"

"Listening at doors," said Green. "And don't say you weren't, because you wouldn't have known we were finished else."

Bella said simply. "Ena has been very interested in your efforts to free Sid Lunn."

"Oh, yes? Is he a friend of hers then?"

"Where else do you think I got those pigeons from that you ate so much of and that hare to put in my deep freeze?" asked Ena Cully pityingly.

THE PERENNIAL LIBRARY MYSTERY SERIES

Delano Ames

CORPSE DIPLOMATIQUE   P 637, $2.84
"Sprightly and intelligent."

—*New York Herald Tribune Book Review*

FOR OLD CRIME'S SAKE   P 629, $2.84

MURDER, MAESTRO, PLEASE   P 630, $2.84
"If there is a more engaging couple in modern fiction than Jane and
Dagobert Brown, we have not met them."   —*Scotsman*

SHE SHALL HAVE MURDER   P 638, $2.84
"Combines the merit of both the English and American schools in the
new mystery. It's as breezy as the best of the American ones, and has
the sophistication and wit of any top-notch Britisher."

—*New York Herald Tribune Book Review*

E. C. Bentley

TRENT'S LAST CASE   P 440, $2.50
"One of the three best detective stories ever written."

—Agatha Christie

TRENT'S OWN CASE   P 516, $2.25
"I won't waste time saying that the plot is sound and the detection
satisfying. Trent has not altered a scrap and reappears with all his old
humor and charm."   —Dorothy L. Sayers

Gavin Black

A DRAGON FOR CHRISTMAS   P 473, $1.95
"Potent excitement!"   —*New York Herald Tribune*

THE EYES AROUND ME   P 485, $1.95
"I stayed up until all hours last night reading *The Eyes Around Me,*
which is something I do not do very often, but I was so intrigued by the
ingeniousness of Mr. Black's plotting and the witty way in which he spins
his mystery. I can only say that I enjoyed the book enormously."

—F. van Wyck Mason

YOU WANT TO DIE, JOHNNY?   P 472, $1.95
"Gavin Black doesn't just develop a pressure plot in suspense, he adds
uninfected wit, character, charm, and sharp knowledge of the Far East
to make rereading as keen as the first race-through."   —*Book Week*

Nicholas Blake

THE CORPSE IN THE SNOWMAN P 427, $1.95
"If there is a distinction between the novel and the detective story (which we do not admit), then this book deserves a high place in both categories." —*The New York Times*

THE DREADFUL HOLLOW P 493, $1.95
"Pace unhurried, characters excellent, reasoning solid."
—*San Francisco Chronicle*

END OF CHAPTER P 397, $1.95
". . . admirably solid . . . an adroit formal detective puzzle backed up by firm characterization and a knowing picture of London publishing."
—*The New York Times*

HEAD OF A TRAVELER P 398, $2.25
"Another grade A detective story of the right old jigsaw persuasion."
—*New York Herald Tribune Book Review*

MINUTE FOR MURDER P 419, $1.95
"An outstanding mystery novel. Mr. Blake's writing is a delight in itself." —*The New York Times*

THE MORNING AFTER DEATH P 520, $1.95
"One of Blake's best."
—Rex Warner

A PENKNIFE IN MY HEART P 521, $2.25
"Style brilliant . . . and suspenseful." —*San Francisco Chronicle*

THE PRIVATE WOUND P 531, $2.25
[Blake's] best novel in a dozen years . . . . An intensely penetrating study of sexual passion. . . . A powerful story of murder and its aftermath."
—Anthony Boucher, *The New York Times*

A QUESTION OF PROOF P 494, $1.95
"The characters in this story are unusually well drawn, and the suspense is well sustained." —*The New York Times*

THE SAD VARIETY P 495, $2.25
"It is a stunner. I read it instead of eating, instead of sleeping."
—Dorothy Salisbury Davis

THERE'S TROUBLE BREWING P 569, $3.37
"Nigel Strangeways is a puzzling mixture of simplicity and penetration, but all the more real for that." —*The Times Literary Supplement*

THOU SHELL OF DEATH   P 428, $1.95
"It has all the virtues of culture, intelligence and sensibility that the most exacting connoisseur could ask of detective fiction."
          —*The Times* [London] *Literary Supplement*

THE WIDOW'S CRUISE   P 399, $2.25
"A stirring suspense. . . . The thrilling tale leaves nothing to be desired."
          —*Springfield Republican*

THE WORM OF DEATH   P 400, $2.25
"It [The Worm of Death] is one of Blake's very best—and his best is better than almost anyone's."   —Louis Untermeyer

John & Emery Bonett

A BANNER FOR PEGASUS   P 554, $2.40
"A gem! Beautifully plotted and set. . . . Not only is the murder adroit and deserved, and the detection competent, but the love story is charming."   —Jacques Barzun and Wendell Hertig Taylor

DEAD LION   P 563, $2.40
"A clever plot, authentic background and interesting characters highly recommended this one."   —*New Republic*

Christianna Brand

GREEN FOR DANGER   P 551, $2.50
"You have to reach for the greatest of Great Names (Christie, Carr, Queen . . .) to find Brand's rivals in the devious subtleties of the trade."
          —Anthony Boucher

TOUR DE FORCE   P 572, $2.40
"Complete with traps for the over-ingenious, a double-reverse surprise ending and a key clue planted so fairly and obviously that you completely overlook it. If that's your idea of perfect entertainment, then seize at once upon *Tour de Force.*"   —Anthony Boucher, *The New York Times*

James Byrom

OR BE HE DEAD   P 585, $2.84
"A very original tale . . . Well written and steadily entertaining."
          —Jacques Barzun & Wendell Hertig Taylor, *A Catalogue of Crime*

Henry Calvin

IT'S DIFFERENT ABROAD   P 640, $2.84

"What is remarkable and delightful, Mr. Calvin imparts a flavor of satire to what he renovates and compels us to take straight."

—Jacques Barzun

Marjorie Carleton

VANISHED   P 559, $2.40

"Exceptional . . . a minor triumph."

—Jacques Barzun and Wendell Hertig Taylor, *A Catalogue of Crime*

George Harmon Coxe

MURDER WITH PICTURES   P 527, $2.25

"[Coxe] has hit the bull's-eye with his first shot."

—*The New York Times*

Edmund Crispin

BURIED FOR PLEASURE   P 506, $2.50

"Absolute and unalloyed delight." .

—Anthony Boucher, *The New York Times*

Lionel Davidson

THE MENORAH MEN   P 592, $2.84

"Of his fellow thriller writers, only John Le Carré shows the same instinct for the viscera."   —*Chicago Tribune*

NIGHT OF WENCESLAS   P 595, $2.84

"A most ingenious thriller, so enriched with style, wit, and a sense of serious comedy that it all but transcends its kind."

—*The New Yorker*

THE ROSE OF TIBET   P 593, $2.84

"I hadn't realized how much I missed the genuine Adventure story . . . until I read *The Rose of Tibet*."   —Graham Greene

D. M. Devine

MY BROTHER'S KILLER   P 558, $2.40

"A most enjoyable crime story which I enjoyed reading down to the last moment."   —Agatha Christie

THE DANGER WITHIN   P 448, $1.95
"Michael Gilbert has nicely combined some elements of the straight
detective story with plenty of action, suspense, and adventure, to produce a superior thriller."   —*Saturday Review*

FEAR TO TREAD   P 458, $1.95
"Merits serious consideration as a work of art."
                                        —*The New York Times*

Joe Gores

HAMMETT   P 631, $2.84
"Joe Gores at his very best. Terse, powerful writing—with the master,
Dashiell Hammett, as the protagonist in a novel I think he would have
been proud to call his own."   —Robert Ludlum

C. W. Grafton

BEYOND A REASONABLE DOUBT   P 519, $1.95
"A very ingenious tale of murder . . . a brilliant and gripping narrative."
                            —Jacques Barzun and Wendell Hertig Taylor

THE RAT BEGAN TO GNAW THE ROPE   P 639, $2.84
"Fast, humorous story with flashes of brilliance."
                                        —*The New Yorker*

Edward Grierson

THE SECOND MAN   P 528, $2.25
"One of the best trial-testimony books to have come along in quite a
while."   —*The New Yorker*

Bruce Hamilton

TOO MUCH OF WATER   P 635, $2.84
"A superb sea mystery. . . . The prose is excellent."
        —Jacques Barzun and Wendell Hertig Taylor, *A Catalogue of Crime*

Cyril Hare

DEATH IS NO SPORTSMAN   P 555, $2.40
"You will be thrilled because it succeeds in placing an ingenious story
in a new and refreshing setting. . . . The identity of the murderer is really
a surprise."   —*Daily Mirror*

Cyril Hare (cont'd)

DEATH WALKS THE WOODS P 556, $2.40

"Here is a fine formal detective story, with a technically brilliant solution demanding the attention of all connoisseurs of construction."

—Anthony Boucher, *The New York Times Book Review*

AN ENGLISH MURDER P 455, $2.50

"By a long shot, the best crime story I have read for a long time. Everything is traditional, but originality does not suffer. The setting is perfect. Full marks to Mr. Hare." —*Irish Press*

SUICIDE EXCEPTED P 636, $2.84

"Adroit in its manipulation . . . and distinguished by a plot-twister which I'll wager Christie wishes she'd thought of."

—*The New York Times*

TENANT FOR DEATH P 570, $2.84

"The way in which an air of probability is combined both with clear, terse narrative and with a good deal of subtle suburban atmosphere, proves the extreme skill of the writer." —*The Spectator*

TRAGEDY AT LAW P 522, $2.25

"An extremely urbane and well-written detective story."

—*The New York Times*

UNTIMELY DEATH P 514, $2.25

"The English detective story at its quiet best, meticulously underplayed, rich in perceivings of the droll human animal and ready at the last with a neat surprise which has been there all the while had we but wits to see it." —*New York Herald Tribune Book Review*

THE WIND BLOWS DEATH P 589, $2.84

"A plot compounded of musical knowledge, a Dickens allusion, and a subtle point in law is related with delightfully unobtrusive wit, warmth, and style." —*The New York Times*

WITH A BARE BODKIN P 523, $2.25

"One of the best detective stories published for a long time."

—*The Spectator*

Robert Harling

THE ENORMOUS SHADOW P 545, $2.50

"In some ways the best spy story of the modern period. . . . The writing is terse and vivid . . . the ending full of action . . . altogether first-rate."
—Jacques Barzun and Wendell Hertig Taylor, *A Catalogue of Crime*

Matthew Head

THE CABINDA AFFAIR   P 541, $2.25
"An absorbing whodunit and a distinguished novel of atmosphere."
                                    —Anthony Boucher, *The New York Times*

THE CONGO VENUS   P 597, $2.84
"Terrific. The dialogue is just plain wonderful."
                                              —*The Boston Globe*

MURDER AT THE FLEA CLUB   P 542, $2.50
"The true delight is in Head's style, its limpid ease combined with humor
and an awesome precision of phrase."   —*San Francisco Chronicle*

M. V. Heberden

ENGAGED TO MURDER   P 533, $2.25
"Smooth plotting."   —*The New York Times*

James Hilton

WAS IT MURDER?   P 501, $1.95
"The story is well planned and well written."
                                              —*The New York Times*

P. M. Hubbard

HIGH TIDE   P 571, $2.40
"A smooth elaboration of mounting horror and danger."
                                              —*Library Journal*

Elspeth Huxley

THE AFRICAN POISON MURDERS   P 540, $2.25
"Obscure venom, manical mutilations, deadly bush fire, thrilling climax
compose major opus.... Top-flight."
                                    —*Saturday Review of Literature*

MURDER ON SAFARI   P 587, $2.84
"Right now we'd call Mrs. Huxley a dangerous rival to Agatha Christie."   —*Books*

Francis Iles

BEFORE THE FACT   P 517, $2.50
"Not many 'serious' novelists have produced character studies to compare with Iles's internally terrifying portrait of the murderer in *Before the Fact*, his masterpiece and a work truly deserving the appellation of unique and beyond price."   —Howard Haycraft

MALICE AFORETHOUGHT   P 532, $1.95
"It is a long time since I have read anything so good as *Malice Aforethought*, with its cynical humour, acute criminology, plausible detail and rapid movement. It makes you hug yourself with pleasure."
           —H. C. Harwood, *Saturday Review*

Michael Innes

THE CASE OF THE JOURNEYING BOY   P 632, $3.12
"I could see no faults in it. There is no one to compare with him."
           —*Illustrated London News*

DEATH BY WATER   P 574, $2.40
"The amount of ironic social criticism and deft characterization of scenes and people would serve another author for six books."
           —Jacques Barzun and Wendell Hertig Taylor

HARE SITTING UP   P 590, $2.84
"There is hardly anyone (in mysteries or mainstream) more exquisitely literate, allusive and Jamesian—and hardly anyone with a firmer sense of melodramatic plot or a more vigorous gift of storytelling."
           —Anthony Boucher, *The New York Times*

THE LONG FAREWELL   P 575, $2.40
"A model of the deft, classic detective story, told in the most wittily diverting prose."   —*The New York Times*

THE MAN FROM THE SEA   P 591, $2.84
"The pace is brisk, the adventures exciting and excitingly told, and above all he keeps to the very end the interesting ambiguity of the man from the sea."   —*New Statesman*

THE SECRET VANGUARD   P 584, $2.84
"Innes . . . has mastered the art of swift, exciting and well-organized narrative."   —*The New York Times*

THE WEIGHT OF THE EVIDENCE   P 633, $2.84
"First-class puzzle, deftly solved. University background interesting and amusing."   —*Saturday Review of Literature*

Mary Kelly

THE SPOILT KILL   P 565, $2.40
"Mary Kelly is a new Dorothy Sayers. . . . [An] exciting new novel."
                                                    —*Evening News*

Lange Lewis

THE BIRTHDAY MURDER   P 518, $1.95
"Almost perfect in its playlike purity and delightful prose."
                              —Jacques Barzun and Wendell Hertig Taylor

Allan MacKinnon

HOUSE OF DARKNESS   P 582, $2.84
"His best . . . a perfect compendium."
   —Jacques Barzun & Wendell Hertig Taylor, *A Catalogue of Crime*

Arthur Maling

LUCKY DEVIL   P 482, $1.95
"The plot unravels at a fast clip, the writing is breezy and Maling's
approach is as fresh as today's stockmarket quotes."
                                      —*Louisville Courier Journal*

RIPOFF   P 483, $1.95
"A swiftly paced story of today's big business is larded with intrigue as
a Ralph Nader-type investigates an insurance scandal and is soon on the
run from a hired gun and his brother. . . . Engrossing and credible."
                                                    —*Booklist*

SCHROEDER'S GAME   P 484, $1.95
"As the title indicates, this Schroeder is up to something, and the un-
ravelling of his game is a diverting and sufficiently blood-soaked entertainment."   —*The New Yorker*

Austin Ripley

MINUTE MYSTERIES   P 387, $2.50
More than one hundred of the world's shortest detective stories. Only
one possible solution to each case!

Thomas Sterling

THE EVIL OF THE DAY   P 529, $2.50
"Prose as witty and subtle as it is sharp and clear. . .characters unconven-
tionally conceived and richly bodied forth . . . . In short, a novel to be
treasured."   —Anthony Boucher, *The New York Times*

Julian Symons

THE BELTING INHERITANCE P 468, $1.95
"A superb whodunit in the best tradition of the detective story."
—August Derleth, *Madison Capital Times*

BLAND BEGINNING P 469, $1.95
"Mr. Symons displays a deft storytelling skill, a quiet and literate wit, a nice feeling for character, and detectival ingenuity of a high order."
—Anthony Boucher, *The New York Times*

BOGUE'S FORTUNE P 481, $1.95
"There's a touch of the old sardonic humour, and more than a touch of style." —*The Spectator*

THE BROKEN PENNY P 480, $1.95
"The most exciting, astonishing and believable spy story to appear in years. —Anthony Boucher, *The New York Times Book Review*

THE COLOR OF MURDER P 461, $1.95
"A singularly unostentatious and memorably brilliant detective story."
—*New York Herald Tribune Book Review*

Dorothy Stockbridge Tillet
(John Stephen Strange)

THE MAN WHO KILLED FORTESCUE P 536, $2.25
"Better than average." —*Saturday Review of Literature*

Simon Troy

THE ROAD TO RHUINE P 583, $2.84
"Unusual and agreeably told." —*San Francisco Chronicle*

SWIFT TO ITS CLOSE P 546, $2.40
"A nicely literate British mystery . . . the atmosphere and the plot are exceptionally well wrought, the dialogue excellent." —*Best Sellers*

Henry Wade

THE DUKE OF YORK'S STEPS P 588, $2.84
"A classic of the golden age."
—Jacques Barzun & Wendell Hertig Taylor, *A Catalogue of Crime*

A DYING FALL P 543, $2.50
"One of those expert British suspense jobs . . . it crackles with undercurrents of blackmail, violent passion and murder. Topnotch in its class."
—*Time*

If you enjoyed this book you'll want to know about THE PERENNIAL LIBRARY MYSTERY SERIES

Buy them at your local bookstore or use this coupon for ordering:

Qty	P number	Price
_____	_____	_____
_____	_____	_____
_____	_____	_____
_____	_____	_____
_____	_____	_____
_____	_____	_____
_____	_____	_____
_____	_____	_____
_____	_____	_____
_____	_____	_____
_____	_____	_____
_____	_____	_____
_____	_____	_____
_____	_____	_____

postage and handling charge $1.00
_____ book(s) @ $0.25   _____

TOTAL   ⬜

Prices contained in this coupon are Harper & Row invoice prices only. They are subject to change without notice, and in no way reflect the prices at which these books may be sold by other suppliers.

HARPER & ROW, Mail Order Dept. #PMS, 10 East 53rd St., New York, N.Y. 10022.

Please send me the books I have checked above. I am enclosing $_____ which includes a postage and handling charge of $1.00 for the first book and 25¢ for each additional book. Send check or money order. No cash or C.O.D.s please

Name_____

Address_____

City_____ State_____ Zip_____

Please allow 4 weeks for delivery. USA only. This offer expires 9/30/84. Please add applicable sales tax.